11-21-10

DATE DUE

DEC 0 5 2010			

DEMCO 38-297

Easy Avenue

Easy Avenue

BRIAN DOYLE

A Groundwood Book

Douglas & McIntyre

TORONTO / VANCOUVER / BUFFALO

Groundwood Books / Douglas & McIntyre Ltd.
585 Bloor Street West, Toronto, Ontario M6G 1K5

Distributed in the USA by Publishers Group West
1700 Fourth Street, Berkeley, CA 94710

We acknowledge the financial support of the Canada Council for
the Arts, the Ontario Arts Council and the Government of Canada
through the Book Publishing Industry Development Program for
our publishing activities.

Library of Congress data is available

Canadian Cataloguing in Publication Data

Doyle, Brian   .
Easy Avenue

"A Groundwood book."
ISBN 0-88899-338-2

PS8557.087E28 1998   jC813'.54   C88-094544-3
PZ7.D69Ea 1998

Design by Michael Solomon
Cover illustration by Ludmilla Temertey
Printed and bound in Canada by Webcom

To Fay, John, Jo, Kelly,
Tobias, Eliza, John Peter,
Wylie and Gabriel

And to Mike, Jenny, Sarah,
Moira, Simon and Rowan

And to Jackie, Megan and Ryan

CONTENTS

1

The World's Worst Golfer

My last name is O'Driscoll and my first name is Hulbert. When I was little I couldn't say the word Hulbert very well. The word Hulbert came out something like Hubbo, and everybody started calling me that. They still call me that. Hubbo. Hubbo O'Driscoll.

There were lots of O'Driscolls in Lowertown, Ottawa. There was the O'Driscoll who was a policeman who took his holidays around Christmas so he could work at playing Santa Claus at Woolworth's on Rideau Street.

He's not in this story.

There were other people in Lowertown that you might know. Tommy, I don't know his last name, who thought he was The Shadow. He's not in this story either. Well, maybe he is, once. And Killer Bodnoff.

And Fleurette Featherstone Fitchell. You might know her. You might have heard of her. She *is* in this story.

My first memory about moving from Lowertown to our new place to live at the Uplands Emergency Shelter is not about moving there or about the bus to get out there, but it is about a place right next to Uplands Emergency Shelter. The golf course.

The Ottawa Hunt and Golf Club, where I got a job caddying just a few days after we moved near there in the summer.

And where something happened.

Everybody in the Uplands Emergency Shelter was poor, and of course everybody at the Ottawa Hunt and Golf Club was rich, except the caddies.

We made seventy-five cents for caddying eighteen holes. And maybe a tip. I was one of the lucky ones though; I made a dollar fifty for eighteen holes because I was Mr. Donald D. DonaldmcDonald's special caddy. Nobody wanted to caddy for Mr. Donald D. DonaldmcDonald because he was such a rotten golfer and he had such a vicious temper. His face would get red and his eyes would begin to bulge out when his ball would take off into the bush, which was practically every time he hit it. And he would often throw his club into the bush too. I would have to go and get it and also find his ball for him.

His ball would be so far into the bush that I'd either never find it or if I did it would be in a hopeless place and he'd get mad all over again.

I used to find a lot of other golf balls while I was in there looking for Mr. Donald D. DonaldmcDonald's ball, and when I'd find one that was his brand I'd keep it so that sometimes I'd be able to drop one in not a bad place alongside the fairway in the rough grass and tell him it was his so he'd have a shot at it without taking a penalty.

He always played alone and even though he yelled and screamed almost all the way over the eighteen holes I knew he wasn't mad at me; he was mad at the golf bag, the ball, the clubs, the golf course, the trees, the bunkers, the rocks, the bushes, the water, the greens, the tee, the pin and himself.

He didn't seem to have any friends. Except maybe me.

10

Sometimes when we'd be waiting for other golfers and there was nothing to do I would practice my handstand and my round-off back handspring. He used to like that. It even made him smile sometimes.

He played two rounds every Saturday and two rounds every Sunday. And I was his personal caddy.

He said he played to let off steam.

Letting off steam meant that all week steam would build up inside him (not real steam) and on the weekends he'd have to let it out or he would explode.

The last time I ever caddied for him something bad happened.

I came out of the bush with one of his golf clubs and got a funny feeling that something was wrong. I couldn't see him anywhere.

Then I saw two golf shoes, the toes pointing into the ground behind the ball washer. There were legs attached to the shoes.

When I got to him his fingers were clawing the grass and his mouth was sucking in dirt. The back of his neck and his ears were bluish grey.

His golf bag was lying a few steps away where he had been trying to tee off. That's why I didn't see him fall. I was in the bush looking for one of his golf clubs that he threw in there after his first bad shot.

I unzipped the pocket of the bag where I knew he kept those pills. I knew everything he had in his bag because he'd get me to try and tidy it up after the first nine holes each time while he went into the clubhouse for something to drink and to relax.

He had to go in to let off some more steam.

His bag was always a wreck because of all the things he did to it when he was mad, which was most of the time.

Jumping up and down on your golf bag with those spiked shoes isn't good for it. Jumping up and down with both feet scars and tears the leather of a golf

11

bag. And kicking it along the fairway. And throwing your golf bag into creeks and mud holes is bad for it. And so is swinging your golf bag by the strap with both hands, beating it against rough pine-tree trunks. And throwing it into sand traps. And lifting very heavy rocks over your head and crushing your golf bag with those rocks.

Or using your golf club like an axe and chopping your golf bag. He did these things all the time.

He would hit his ball as hard as he could and the ball would head right for the bush, bounce off a tree, and disappear. Or he would try to hit the ball and it would dribble just a few yards away.

Then he would attack the bag.

Then I would pick it up and carry it to where his ball was (unless it was in the bush) and give him his next club and he would try again. Then he would probably hit the ball on the very top and it would fly straight up in the air and come back down almost in the same place and then he'd throw his club away over into the bush and while I ran to get it he would attack the bag again.

He never got mad at me. Usually the bag.

This was why I knew everything about his golf bag. Each time he went into the clubhouse to let off steam I would work on the bag. Get it back in shape. I would clean it off with a rag and soap and water and then while it was drying I would go through the pockets cleaning out the mud and sand and broken trees and stuff. And I'd rub the bag down with protective wax and maybe put some shellac I'd get from the pro shop on the gashes and cuts in the leather.

He had his name printed inside a little plastic window on the bag. Mr. Donald D. Donaldmc-Donald. Sometimes I'd say it over like a little song:

Donald D. DonaldmcDonald,
Donald D. DonaldmcDonald,
Donald D. Donald,
Donald D. Donald,
Donald D. DonaldmcDonald.

I was pretty good at saying it. I was a much better pronouncer than I was when I was little and couldn't even say Hulbert.

And I always wanted to ask him what his initial D. stood for, but I never did.

As I was saying, I knew his golf bag very well. That's why I knew what those pills were and what they were for. It said so right on the bottle. He was lying there on his stomach with his face in the grass. His fingers were out like claws, clawing the grass like our cat used to claw the blanket on the bed down in Lowertown. The back of his neck and his cheeks were a bluish grey colour.

There was nobody around and the golf course was as quiet as a graveyard. A squirrel bounced up to us and stopped to watch. I got out the bottle of pills from the bag and twisted off the top. The little sign on the bottle said, "Place glycerine pill under tongue. If mouth dry moisten with drops of water."

There was a tap sticking up out of the grass down by the ladies' tee. I ran down there and turned on the tap and cupped my hands under it. The water was gushing out so fast I couldn't get much to stay in my hands. I ran back up to him holding my hands high out in front of me. There wasn't much left when I got there but there was enough to wet his mouth. I looked around on the grass where I left the pills. They weren't there. I crawled around slapping the grass looking for the bottle. I looked up and saw the squirrel hopping away with it in his mouth. I let out a yell and he dropped it and bounced away a few times and stopped. A bold little guy. I crawled over monkey style and got the bottle.

Mr. Donald D. DonaldmcDonald gave out a long groan to me as I shoved a pill under his tongue with my finger.

I got out some driver covers and made a little pillow for the side of his head so his mouth wouldn't roll back into the grass. I looked to see if anybody was around to help.

The squirrel was sitting up, still as a statue, watching. The heat bugs were singing.

I looked down the fairway to see how far I'd have to run to the clubhouse. He gave out another long groan and his throat muscles started working.

I ran as fast as I could down the fairway and cut across to the first tee. In the clubhouse I explained what happened between breaths. They called an ambulance and we jumped on the sod truck and drove right down the middle of the fairway to where he was. When we got there he was trying to sit up. His face was white but not bluish anymore, and his eyes were fuzzy and unfocused. We helped him onto some sod on the back of the truck and I threw his clubs on and we drove off.

We met the ambulance halfway up the fairway and the men put him on their stretcher and slid him into the back of the ambulance.

I told them about the pill.

"Lucky for him you knew about the pills," one of the ambulance guys said. "Probably saved his life."

As they were putting him in the ambulance, tucking in his blanket, his eyes got a bit clear and he looked right at me. With his free arm Mr. Donald D. DonaldmcDonald reached over and weakly squeezed me on the shoulder.

Then they shut the door and drove off with the siren crying.

14

I reached up and touched my shoulder where Mr. Donald D. DonaldmcDonald squeezed it a bit to see what he had felt there. How it felt to him.

I never caddied again.

2
Drowned in the War

M y dad was run over by a streetcar. He lay down
on the streetcar tracks for a rest during a snow-
storm. The driver couldn't see very well because of
the blowing snow and ran over him. I never knew
him because that happened when I was just a baby.

My mom died when I was born.

I guess you could say I was kind of an orphan.

I lived with Mrs. O'Driscoll. She was married to
a distant cousin of my dad's. I thought of her as my
mother and I loved her and at school and every-
where I said she was my mother but at home I always
called her Mrs. O'Driscoll. It was a warm little joke
we had between us.

After we moved to Uplands Emergency Shelter
Mrs. O'Driscoll got a job as a cleaning lady at Glebe
Collegiate Institute. Glebe Collegiate Institute was
a big high school in the southern part of Ottawa.
The high school where I would go that fall.

Mrs. O'Driscoll's husband, Mr. O'Driscoll, was
drowned in the war. In the Pacific Ocean. Mr.
O'Driscoll was a wild kind of man with red hair and
freckles on the backs of his hands and on his neck.
He laughed a lot and he liked making jokes. Bad
jokes.

The day he drowned he was talking with a man,
making jokes and rolling a cigarette in the front part

of the ship, on the main deck. Suddenly there was a dull sort of a thud and the horns started going and the ship started sinking.

The man who was rolling the cigarette shook hands with Mr. O'Driscoll and they said good-bye, they'd see each other later, and they both jumped in the water. One over one side of the boat and one over the other side.

The man rolling the cigarette got saved and came around to our house after the war and told us all about it.

Mr. O'Driscoll didn't get saved.

Just before he jumped overboard, Mr. O'Driscoll yelled out to his friend, "If I don't see you in the spring, I'll see you in the mattress!"

As you can see, Mr. O'Driscoll was quite a funny guy.

It was a joke mixing up spring, the season, with the spring in a bed. I guess it would be something one bedbug would say to another bedbug. Maybe Mr. O'Driscoll mentioned the bedbugs but the wind was howling too loud or there were too many explosions and things and the man rolling the cigarette didn't hear that part.

I remember when the man came to see us and tell us about Mr. O'Driscoll's last moments. We already knew how drowned he was because of the letter Mrs. O'Driscoll got from the government. The letter said he was "missing."

After she opened it and read it she said, "He never was much of a swimmer." She said this the way she said everything. Out of the side of her mouth. Then she cried for about three days.

When the friend showed up a few months later he had trouble finding us.

We lived in Building Number Eight, Unit B, Uplands Emergency Shelter.

We had to move there from Lowertown because of the housing shortage after the war. The person who owned our house on St. Patrick Street in Lowertown sold it to somebody and we had to move out.

He came over to our house at the end of June on my last day of public school at York Street and told us. I came down St. Patrick Street with all my books and my report that said I passed, On Condition, and there he was, standing on the steps, talking to Mrs. O'Driscoll, telling her that we had to get out.

On Condition meant if you didn't do very well in grade nine, they'd send you back to grade eight. I wasn't a very good student.

"I suppose you know what you can do with your house," I heard Mrs. O'Driscoll say to the man out of the corner of her mouth. But she saved the *very* corner of her mouth for special occasions.

She looked around for another place to live in Lowertown, but there weren't any. Finally, in July, she told me.

"We're going to Uplands Emergency Shelter," she said. "It's an air force base about ten miles south of Ottawa. Uplands Emergency Shelter." She said "Emergency Shelter" out of such a tight corner of her mouth that I could hardly understand it at first.

But the tightest corner of her mouth I *ever* heard her use was the corner she used when I told her about the mysterious money I was getting from somewhere.

"Mysterious money?" she said.

But that was after school started.

3

Fleurette Featherstone Fitchell

A ll summer, families with nowhere to live were moving into Uplands Emergency Shelter.

Families with screaming babies and piles of brothers and sisters and broken trucks and torn furniture and tubs full of junk and mop handles pointing out and pails with leftover food and blankets tied with rope and bent beds and stained mattresses and ice boxes with the doors hanging and bureaus stuck in passageways and fat tires and homemade shelves and cracked dishes and three-legged chairs and twisted curtain rods and coiled springs sticking out of ripped sofas and yelling and swearing.

The mother of the new family moving into our building had a black eye and a cast on her wrist. She wouldn't look at anybody.

I recognized the girl carrying in the broken lamp. I asked her if she wanted some help and she said no. She had black curly long hair tied at the back with a white rag. She had brown-black eyes and long black eyelashes and very white skin.

She didn't say no in a mean way but you knew that she meant it. She wasn't just being polite or shy or proud or anything like that. You could tell that she just meant no.

I remembered her from York Street School. I was never in her class but I remembered that Killer

19

Bodnoff and some of the guys would sneak over into the girls' schoolyard and chase her and her friends and throw snow at them and try to kiss them. Killer used to say that she would even take guys into her back shed with her on Friel Street. He used to call it *Feel* Street. He used to say that she was dirty.

Her name was Fleurette Featherstone Fitchell.

Later that day I was lined up at the toilet with some of the other people in our building — Mr. Blank, his strange little dog Nerves, Mr. Yasso, Mrs. Quirk and her boy with no brain and, behind me, my new neighbour.

"Is this the only toilet?" she said. "For six families?"

"Eight," I said. "There are eight families. Two for each part of the H. You are the eighth family to move in," I said. She looked at me.

"You went to York Street School," she said. "Can you still stand on your hands?" She was looking right at me from out of her brown-black eyes.

I did a perfect handstand while the little dog, Nerves, came around and stared in my face so that I started to laugh and had to come down.

"Your name is Hulbert O'Driscoll," she said.

"Hubbo," I said.

"How did you know I could stand on my hands?" I said.

"We used to watch you after school in the gym. Some of the girls really liked you."

"Me?" I was so embarrassed that I did another handstand and hand-walked away down the hall so she wouldn't see my face. Nerves clicked down the hall with me, trying to do a paw-stand probably. When I got back and stood up again I said that I knew her too.

"Your name is Fleurette Featherstone Fitchell. Everybody knew you." As soon as I said that I knew I shouldn't have. All of a sudden I felt awful.

The toilet was free now and I was next.

"Would you like to go first?" I said, being a big gentleman.

"No." Not polite, not shy, not proud. Just no.

I went in and shut the door.

I didn't want her to hear me going so I turned on the tap.

When I came out Fleurette and Nerves were staring at each other. A staring match.

"Is this a real dog or what is it?" said Fleurette Featherstone Fitchell. Then she went in the toilet and shut the door.

She didn't turn on the tap. I went down the hall to my unit with Nerves, who walked along beside me taking little glances at me as we moved along. Nerves was a little dog that looked a lot like a rat. His tail was like a little black whip and his body was fat and pulpy-looking and his snout was pointed just like a rat's snout. And when he walked his claws made little clicking noises on the floor. And his little whiskers stuck out like a rat's whiskers. And his eyes were shiny and always darting around and he'd move along a few quick steps going click click and then stop and his ears would stiffen up and his nose would start to move around like a little eraser rubbing out something invisible in the air in front of him. Then he'd click click on a little more.

Whenever Mr. Blank came in the door, Nerves would wait to see what mood he was in and then get in the same mood right away. If Mr. Blank was grumpy or frowning, Nerves would kind of frown and show his pointy little rat's teeth. If Mr. Blank was happy, smiling and feeling good, Nerves would jump up and down and wag his ratty little tail and squeak like a rat laughing.

And if Mr. Blank was thinking about something hard or trying to figure out a crossword puzzle, Nerves would stand there beside him and look down at the floor and sort of study it as if he were studying a speck of dirt or trying to read something that was written there.

Mr. Blank hated Nerves. He hated to come home from work after a tiring day and as soon as he walked in the door have Nerves there, imitating him.

"Why can't we have a normal dog?" Mr. Blank would say to Mrs. Blank. "I hate this dog. Look at him. He's making fun of me. Nerves! Be yourself! Develop a personality of your own! Leave me out of it!"

And Nerves would glare right back at him, doing a perfect imitation of him.

Then Mr. Blank would sit down with the paper in his chair and let out a big sigh and Nerves would get on the other chair and sigh too. A rat's sigh.

And after a while Mr. Blank would look up over his paper and say, "I hate you, Nerves."

And Nerves would show him his little teeth.

And sometimes when Mr. Blank would try to kiss Mrs. Blank or cuddle up to her while she was making the supper, Nerves would be right there beside them with his front paws around Mr. Blank's leg, kissing Mr. Blank's pants with his ratty little tongue.

And then maybe Mr. Blank, just so that he could relax and eat his supper in peace, would put Nerves outside. Then he'd sit down and start to eat and he'd lift up his fork with the spaghetti hanging from it and the fork would stop right about at his open mouth because he'd suddenly see Nerves, outside, staring at him through the window, licking his rodenty little chops and nodding his head as if he were saying, "Good, eh? Is it good? Is it? Is it good? Go ahead. Eat it. It's good! Is it good?"

"I hate that dog," Mr. Blank would say, "I want to take it to the Humane Society and have it executed."

22

"Oh, don't be silly dear," Mrs. Blank would say. "It's only a little dog."

Nerves was almost like a mirror.

Before I went into my unit, Nerves and I looked at each other for a minute. I tried out a silly sentence on him. I said this: "I think I like you, Fleurette Featherstone Fitchell," I said.

Nerves tucked in his chin and looked down at his foot, being very cute and shy.

What a dog.

4
Picnic

The next morning across the parade square in Uplands Emergency Shelter, at the rec hall where the store was, I met her again. She was buying bologna, macaroni and stale bread.

So was I. Except I had to get some eggs and peanut butter too.

Fleurette Featherstone Fitchell said she never tasted peanut butter. I told her it was best if you toasted the stale bread and then spread the peanut butter on the toasted bread and then if you had some honey . . .

Then I realized I was making her feel rotten because she was so poor. But I also felt kind of good and big because I was so rich. Compared to her. Then I hated myself for being so mean. Feeling rich because of peanut butter.

"Did you used to live on Friel Street in Lower-town?" I asked.

"Yes," she said. "I'm glad we moved. I hated it there."

We were walking back across the parade square towards Unit Number Eight. Our building. Our home.

"Killer Bodnoff used to call it *Feel* Street," I said laughing a bit. Fleurette Featherstone Fitchell didn't say anything. She just looked straight ahead.

24

Beside Building Number Eight was Building Number Nine. Somebody else's home. Then Number Ten. Eight more families in there maybe lined up at their toilet. There were many many buildings all the same. All shaped like an H lying flat. In the bar of the H were the tubs and the toilet. In each arm and each leg of the H were two families. Each family had four rooms with walls separating them that didn't reach the ceiling. The four rooms were called units. In the right leg of the lying down H were units A and B. In the right arm of the H were units C and D. Units E and F were in the left leg. G and H in the left arm.

Fleurette Featherstone Fitchell's address was Building Number Eight, Unit H, around the back.

I looked and saw that her eyes were full of tears.

Our square building was bouncing closer to us as we walked across the parade square. The whole peanut butter business was stuck in my mind. Feeling rich over peanut butter. How stupid. And *Feel* Street.

"I hate that stuff about Feel Street," said Fleurette Featherstone Fitchell. "I knew they were going around saying that. I'm glad I moved. Nobody will talk about me here. Because *hardly* anybody knows me here." She looked right at me while we were walking. She looked at me so long that I had to look away. The word "hardly" stayed there in the air like it was printed in a comic book. I almost did a handstand to get away from her eyes but I couldn't because of the eggs and peanut butter and stuff that I was carrying.

You could tell it was going to be a hot day the way the sun was heating up the pavement of the square and the way the air was starting to shimmer, making Building Eight and the other buildings bend like rubber a little bit as they bounced toward us. It was a very big parade square and we walked together with our groceries for a long time without saying anything. Then I said a very smart, a very intelligent thing for a person whose mind was clogged up with peanut butter and rubber buildings.

"Would you like to go on a picnic?" I said.

"Yes," said Fleurette Featherstone Fitchell. "But only if you promise never, ever, to tell anybody about *Feel* Street. Never, ever."

I promised.

I left Mrs. O'Driscoll a note saying I was going to the sandpits for a picnic with my new neighbour. While I was writing the note I laughed to myself a bit imagining her reading it when she got home. She would say "Picnic!" out of the side of her mouth. "Picnic!" Then she would say "Sandpits!" out of an even tighter corner of her mouth.

I packed half a loaf of bread, a knife, a bottle opener, the peanut butter, a small jar of honey, some matches and a blanket.

I knocked on Fleurette Featherstone Fitchell's door and she opened it right away and came out and closed it right away. She didn't want me to look inside.

We walked out the gate and down the road along the edge of the airport and ran a few times to try and get right under the big planes as they came in for a landing flying low across the road so that you could almost reach up and touch them.

Then we went past the Ottawa Hunt and Golf Club parking lot with all the new cars shining in the sun and the golfers chunking their car doors shut and opening and shutting their trunks and walking with their clubs clinking in their squeaky leather bags and the men and women laughing and diamonds flashing.

Further down the road we turned left at Kelly's Inn, a crooked old shack of a store on the edge of the sandpits, and I bought two bottles of cream soda from the old man in there with the cigarette dangling and his torn undershirt.

And behind Kelly's Inn a way, we ducked through some trees lining the old road and suddenly, stretched before us, all the way down to the river, the sandpits. The first pit was huge and I ran down the steep sliding slope, part sideways, part sliding, part stumbling, part flying with huge steps, the sand giving and pouring around my ankles like brown sugar.

At the bottom I looked up at Fleurette Featherstone Fitchell, standing, watching me, her hands on her hips, at the top of the hot sand cliff. I put up my hand to shade my eyes from the sun. She looked about as tall as my thumb away up there.

She untied the white rag from her black curly long hair and started striding, leaping, jumping down the long steep sand toward me, her hair floating and flying and falling around her as she got bigger and bigger.

We climbed up the steep other side, sliding back half a step for every step we took. At the top we sat down in the hot sand to rest. There was a sand gulley that wove around the next two pits down to the Rideau River. It would be cool down there by the water under the trees.

"I want to learn to walk on my hands," she said, after we got our breath.

"Your fingers are like toes," I said. "You press them and lift them just like standing on your own feet to keep your balance. I'll show you when we get down to the river where the ground is harder."

On the shore by the river I collected some dead twigs and sticks and set up the fire ready for a match.

Then I showed her how to get up on her hands against a tree so she wouldn't fall over like all beginners do. You put your hands on the ground near

27

the tree and put one foot in back of the other. You kick your back foot up and lean your shoulders forward and your legs float up over top of you. You keep your legs straight and your toes pointed. Your toenails rest against the tree and you're in your first handstand. Most people can't get up the first few times because they don't remember to lean their shoulders forward.

Fleurette Featherstone Fitchell got it the first time.

Her dress fell down over her and her hair hung down to the ground. All I could see of her was her legs. Her legs were straight and her toes were pointed. The top of her toes pressed against the tree. A perfect first try. She looked like a strange creature, feet-like hands, no head, and long straight white antennae with toes.

Her pants were frayed and raggedy.

"That was the best I've ever seen a beginner do," I said.

While she tried a few more times I put out the blanket, put the match to the fire and sliced two slices of stale bread. Then I got a couple of green sticks and held her slice over the fire until it was brown. Then the other side. While the bread was hot I spread it thick with peanut butter and then poured honey on the top. When I looked back at her she was sitting, leaning against the tree watching me.

I gave her her first ever peanut-butter-and-honey-roasted-open-sandwich and went back and started to make my own. I peeked up and watched her. She started slowly, tasting. Then her bites got a little bigger and she started to eat around the outside, saving the best part, the middle, for the last. I was enjoying watching her so much I didn't realize that my toast was on fire.

After we ate two more and the fire went out I washed the knife off in the river and cleaned up the honey jar and threw the small hard crust of bread that was left to the fish.

"I'm sweltering," Fleurette Featherstone Fitchell said, "I'm going for a swim."

She reached behind under her hair and unbuttoned the back of her dress and pulled it over her head. Her undershirt had a big hole in the back and the bottom of it was in strings.

When she stood up out of the water with her wet hair she looked like a drowned rat. She didn't really but everybody always says that.

"Do I look like a drowned rat?" she said.

"No," I said. "You don't. You look like a girl who just came out of the water."

"Aren't you coming in?" she said. I was sitting on a log cooling off my feet.

"No," I said. "I'm not that hot."

Actually that was a lie.

I didn't want her to see my underwear.

It had holes in it.

On the way home I asked her if she liked the peanut butter and honey thing. I knew she did like it but I asked her anyway. A question I knew the answer to.

"Yes," she said.

Just yes.

Further up the road I asked her what happened to her mother's wrist.

"It was an accident," she said.

At home, in Building Eight, Fleurette went into her unit and I went into the toilet. When I came out I heard her door slam and a man with black hair and dark eyes came down the hall and left the building.

5
Help Wanted

O ne morning in September, a few days before
school started, I was going into Ottawa to spend
the day looking for a part-time job so we could have
some extra money for stuff I might need for school.
Mrs. O'Driscoll was heading out to her new cleaning
job at Glebe Collegiate Institute and we were on
the Uplands bus together.

She was talking again about the prime minister's
house on Laurier Avenue. It used to be Sir Wilfrid
Laurier's house. Prime Minister King was living there
now. She'd been there earlier in the summer applying for a cleaning job but she didn't get the job.
But she couldn't stop talking about it.

"If only O'Driscoll could see that house," said
Mrs. O'Driscoll about her drowned husband. "He'd
just love that house. O'Driscoll always wanted to be
rich you know. Rich was what he wanted. But how
he'd ever be rich is beyond me. He never had two
cents to rub together. That house is just full of mahogany and oak and rugs and gold and silver and
paintings and fancy lights and . . ."

The bus was passing Mooney's Bay and we were
starting to pick up some of the rich people on the
way.

We, the poor people from Uplands, were already
on the bus, taking up half of all the seats, when the

rich people started to get on. They had to come down the aisle, past us, to find places to sit. Some of them tried to stay standing by the driver but he told them to move along and sit down. They had to come and sit beside one of us. They were putting half of their rear ends onto the seat and trying to balance the other halves on their legs in the aisle. Then they got tired and had to shift over a bit closer to us. But they still tried not to touch us and kept their heads in the aisle as much as possible and their noses pointed upwards so they wouldn't be breathing our air.

" . . . and lovely plush sofas," Mrs. O'Driscoll was saying, "and silk cushions and dark stained chairs and rugs all up and down the stairs and carved knobs on the railings and ceiling-high drapes on the leaded windows . . ."

The bus was rocking on down the road and causing the rich people a lot of trouble. They were squeezing their eyes shut and hanging tight to the seat bars.

At Hog's Back some more rich ones got on and tried to stay near the front but the driver told them to move down the aisle too. The bus was getting pretty crowded.

Hog's Back. Not a very nice name for a place for rich people to live. Some of the Uplands people were saying that the *next* stop should be called "Hog's Arse." They were saying it loud just to annoy the rich ones.

Mrs. O'Driscoll was still talking about the Prime Minister's house.

" . . . and three bathrooms and huge big cupboards full of fancy clothes and a big screened-in verandah all around the house with striped awnings all around and a beautiful garden and inside, oh, if O'Driscoll could only see it, inside there's beautiful woven tapestries on the walls and in the bedroom

31

a huge white rug made from a bear with the head still on it and a carved four-poster bed with draw curtains all around . . ."

When we finally got to the Uplands Bus Terminal in Ottawa South the rich people were pretty well trapped. They couldn't get off first because there were piles of people, poor people, falling down the aisle and tumbling out the door and shoving and swearing and clawing their way out.

And they couldn't wait and get off last because the poor people from Uplands who had taken all the window seats wanted to get out and were crawling over the rich people or shoving them into the aisle. Once they were in the aisle it was too late. Everybody was touching the rich people now, putting their sticky hands on their nice coats, tromping all over their nice shiny shoes, breathing bad teeth right into their nice faces, bodies rubbing against their nice bodies, shoulders hitting shoulders, bony knees touching the backs of their nice fat legs.

They were in a panic as they at last got out of the smelly bus and some of them had wide eyes and others were whispering that they had to get a second car because they couldn't stand this any longer.

I walked Mrs. O'Driscoll up to the corner of Grove and Bank Street and waited until her streetcar came to take her to her job. Then I walked up the west side of Bank Street looking for good places to ask for a job. I tried a few drug stores that needed delivery boys but you had to have your own bicycle and that left me out.

I went into the Avalon Theatre but they didn't need any ushers who couldn't afford to buy their own uniforms.

I went into a little restaurant called the Mirror Grill but they already had a dishwasher. The man who smoked a big cigar there, joked with me and bought me a free coke.

I was in the district they called the Glebe and there was a whole lot of Bank Street to go before I got all the way to the Parliament Buildings where it ended. If I stayed on Bank Street I thought I'd get a job for sure.

But I didn't stay. I turned.

I don't know what made me do it, but I turned left off Bank Street and started down First Avenue. The street was cool in the shade of the overhanging trees and it was quiet and cosy, everybody with their own house and their own verandah and their own lawn and their own laneway and balconies and flowers and garages and backyards. And the people seemed so happy fussing with their kids or reading on their verandahs or snipping away at their flower gardens or dragging a hose up the laneway or shining their cars.

And neighbours chatting politely with each other or waving across the street and laughing. And the breadman talking with the maid on the verandah, the breadman with his basket strapped around his neck, his hands resting in the basket. And the smell of the groceries in the back of Devine's green delivery truck, the delivery man whistling, carrying the groceries up to the lady.

And the freshly cut lawns that smelled like the greens at the Ottawa Hunt and Golf Club.

And further down First Avenue the big square red quiet building with the high steps, Carleton College.

And then further, the biggest building on the street. Glebe Collegiate Institute, where Mrs. O'Driscoll was inside, cleaning, and where I would soon go to school.

I passed the school and the huge schoolyard, a block long, and crossed Bronson Avenue down Carling Avenue hill to Preston Street.

I turned right on Preston Street and tried a store and a bakery but they didn't need anybody — at least I think that's what they said because it was in Italian. I tried the Pure Spring soft drink company but the man there asked me how much I weighed. I wasn't heavy enough to work there. He was a huge man and it would be a hundred years before I weighed as much as he did.

"Put on some pounds and come back and see us," he said, and gave out a big laugh that just about blew me out the door.

Further down Preston Street I saw a church with a sign that said Lutheran and some other things on it. In Lowertown it was mostly Catholic churches and synagogues. I had never heard of a Lutheran church before.

I turned off Preston and went right on Somerset Street. Halfway up the hill I went into a pool hall that had a Help Wanted sign in the window. A French kid about my age was dusting the lampshades over a table. I thought I recognized him from Lowertown. I think his name was CoCo.

"You're too late, my fren'. I jus' got de job one hour ago! Tough luck, eh?"

Further up Somerset I saw a sign in the window of the Cinderella Book Store. "Student Wanted — part time." A feeling of excitement came over me. My heart started to beat faster. I looked in the window for a while pretending I was looking at the books there. I was really looking at my reflection, thinking about what I was going to say. I had a feeling I was going to get this job.

The man inside had thick glasses and hardly any face. He had a face all right, but it was so round and big and flabby that you could hardly see where his nose and his mouth started and where his cheeks ended. It seemed like a blur. And his glasses were so thick you couldn't see his eyes at all. He seemed like a kind man and he spoke in a soft, understanding voice.

We talked about what experience I had working in book stores, which I lied about, the books I'd read, which I didn't lie about.

Then he took out an application form and got my name.

"Hubbo?" he said.

"Actually, it's Hulbert," I said.

"I bet when you were small you couldn't say Hulbert so you said Hubbo and then everybody started calling you Hubbo," he said.

I wondered how he knew that.

My address. Uplands Emergency Shelter, Building Eight, Unit B.

He looked at me a long time after he wrote it down.

Phone? No phone. He drew a dash in the space and looked at me a long time again. My feeling of excitement was gone. I was now feeling nervous. I couldn't think straight. There was panic in me.

Religion? Religion. My mind was a blank. His face was looking like a pudding. If I could only see his eyes. I was trying to think of a religion that he would like. He didn't like the address. He didn't like the blank phone number. He probably knew I lied about my age. I had no experience working in book stores. I had to please him. I concentrated so hard trying to think of a good religion, one that he'd like. I could feel my face getting red. I felt like I was sitting on the toilet.

Then it came to me. The church I had seen down on Preston Street. Maybe that was the church he went to. It was in his part of Ottawa. The sign came up in my imagination in front of me. It was a bit blurry but I thought I could see it. I would try it. I would tell him that was my religion.

"Lithuanian!" I said. I felt like I was on a radio quiz program and I just got the grand prize question. I could hear the bells going and the applause.

Lithuanian.

A Lithuanian is a guy from a country somewhere in Europe called Lithuania.

No wonder he said thank-you but that he didn't think he needed anybody right now.

I was all the way down to the corner of Somerset and Bank Street when I realized how stupid he must have thought I was.

I didn't blame him.

I wouldn't hire me either if I acted like that.

The rest of that side of Bank Street took me until noon. I listened to the big clock on the Peace Tower gong twelve times and then I walked out on Nepean Point to watch the Ottawa River from away up high. The tug boats working the logs down there looked like toys and the logs looked like matchsticks. I was feeling pretty lonesome and small so I went up to the statue of Champlain Holding His Astrolab and sat down at his feet and ate the lunch Mrs. O'Driscoll had made for me. Like I told Mrs. O'Driscoll later, I lunched with Sam Champlain. He's pretty good company for lunch, especially if you're feeling lonesome and small.

After lunch with Sam I worked my way all the way down the other side of Bank Street, asking in about a hundred places for a part-time job. By the time I got back down to Ottawa South and the Up-lands Bus Terminal I was pretty discouraged.

Nobody wanted to hire me.

It was six o'clock and the bus terminal was pretty crowded. Soon I spotted Mrs. O'Driscoll pushing her way through the crowd towards me.

There were about fifteen rich people standing near the door of the bus terminal, trying to keep as far away from us poor people as they could. They had on their nice suits and good shoes and fancy hats and even summer gloves some of them. When I first went in the bus terminal and walked by where they were standing I could smell their perfume and the newness and the richness of their clothes and the leather of some of their purses.

They stood near the door so that when the bus came they could get on first, sit together near the front, and then get off at their rich houses first, without having to pass by or go near the rest of us. They were very quiet and they seemed to stare straight ahead. Now and then, if they said anything to each other, they said it in a kind of whisper through their teeth and without moving their lips very much or turning to look at each other with their eyes. It looked like what they said was really important.

And if they had parcels or bags or purses they hung onto them and hugged them to their bodies as tight as they could, and they stood with their feet tight together so that they took up as little room in the bus terminal as possible.

Mrs. O'Driscoll was telling me more about Prime Minister King's house.

" . . . and he's got a nice big painting of his mother up on the third floor in his study. He's got a light lit in front of it at all times — night and day. The lady in the painting is very beautiful. They say he talks to the painting sometimes. He talks to the picture of his mother. He calls her my lovely mother . . . . And his dog Pat. They say he talks to him too. It's a terrier. Cute little thing. Sometimes he talks to his mother about Pat. Sometimes he'll say, Mother, Pat and I think this or Pat and I think that . . . . And they say he visits with dead people at night. They sit around a table in the dark and he talks to dead President Roosevelt and dead Sir Wilfrid and his dead grandaddy the Lyon. And they told me that an old lady sometimes comes over in the middle of the night with a silver trumpet and voices of the dead speak through the trumpet . . . . O'Driscoll would say that he's crazier than a bag of hammers but who's to know these days . . . ."

On the bus some of the poor people were drunk and laughing very loud and throwing bottles out the windows onto the highway. Some of the women were screaming and fighting with other women and everybody was lighting up cigarettes.

Then the driver said to put out those cigarettes, there is no smoking on the bus, and then everything got very quiet but the cigarettes didn't go out and the rich people in the front of the bus sank down in their seats because they were afraid of what was coming and the driver said again to put out those cigarettes and there was some giggling from some of the women and then some man in a big deep rough voice full of gravel and phlegm said, "Come back here and make me!"

By this time the driver had stopped the bus in the middle of the highway and the rich people were saying oh please and the driver took up a bat from under his seat and went back to the back of the bus and there was an olympic swearing contest and I heard two or three whacks and a lot of screaming and clothes ripping and the rich people at the front were saying oh my god and the driver went back to his seat, wiped the juice off of his bat, checked his mirror to straighten his tie, and started the bus moving again along the highway until he stopped a few times to let the rich people off at their stops.

And the poor people were saying to them as they got off, "Goodnight now, and do have an *awfully* lovely eveningggg!" and then they added some long dirty names that even Mrs. O'Driscoll had never heard before.

"I wish we were rich," I said to Mrs. O'Driscoll when things quietened down a bit.

"What on earth for?" said Mrs. O'Driscoll, out of the corner of her mouth. "This is fun!"

Then she looked at me and got a warm soft look on her face.

"You had a disappointing day, didn't you, Hubbo, my boy," she said.

"I guess so," I said.

"Well," said Mrs. O'Driscoll, "Maybe you *will* be rich someday. But I'm telling you, if you care *too* much about it, you won't be any happier than you are now."

6
Betrayed at the Glebe Collegiate Institute

O n the Uplands bus on our way to our first day
at school one of the Uplands kids who smoked
pushed a lit cigarette into a rich kid's sandwich in
her lunch box when she wasn't looking. There was
some crying and complaining and some of the older
kids at the back were doing volcano burps just to
make the people getting on at Mooney's Bay and
Hog's Back more disgusted.

We got off the bus at the terminal in Ottawa South
and were pretty excited as we walked up Bank Street
and over the Bank Street Bridge. We stopped at the
top of the bridge and leaned over to look down at
the Rideau Canal and the cars on the driveway running along beside it. It was a beautiful September
day, the morning sun making diamonds on the water
down the canal a bit, and some early fallen leaves
floating. The canal was curved away up towards
Bronson Bridge one way, lined with trees hanging
over and beautiful houses half showing behind them.
The other way it curved down past Lansdowne Park
and around towards the Parliament Buildings that
you couldn't see. The football grandstand made a
long shadow across the grass in the sun and the
green wooden fence around the field looked shiny
because of some of the light.

A boy named Denny, who was covered with pimples, and I and Fleurette walked together down the rest of the bridge while the other kids from Uplands came behind us in small groups.

The rich kids were ahead of us in one big group.

Denny and Fleurette and I walked up Bank Street past the Exhibition Grounds and the Avenues and turned left on First Avenue. We strolled down First, looking at the beautiful lawns and the trees and the fancy houses with the big verandahs and the windows with the fat cats sunning themselves and the shiny cars in the laneways.

At the school there was a big crowd of kids standing around waiting for the doors to open. Somebody told Fleurette that the High School of Commerce was at the other end, a long block away, and I said I'd see her later.

I walked up the sloping driveway to look at the front entrance. I stood back and looked at the wide steps and the huge doors. Above the doors carved in stone was a giant shield and a hand holding a flaming torch. There were words underneath.

Alere Flammam.

I walked up the steps and turned around with my back to the doors. A feeling of excitement and great power filled me. I could feel the building behind me. Solid. Important.

I wondered what *Alere Flammam* meant.

I was alone. Everybody else was down the sloping driveway standing around on First Avenue. Many of them were looking up at me alone at the top of the wide steps. Some were pointing. For a minute I felt like an emperor, standing on the great entrance to my palace, surveying my subjects.

I put my hands down on the cool concrete and kicked up into a perfect stand.

I could hear the hooting and whistling from the crowd. I jammed my pointed toes together and secretly pressed and released my fingers on the concrete to keep my balance. I was still as a statue. Somewhere, way above me, was the shield and the flame. My eyes were on a leaf lying on the bottom step below me. I didn't dare look anywhere else in case I'd ruin my handstand. It was perfect. I could have held it for hours.

Suddenly something was wrong. The noise the crowd was making had changed. They weren't hooting and whistling and clapping any more. They were saying something else.

Then I heard a big door click shut and I felt someone behind me. Then my hair was grabbed and the back of my shirt. I was lifted right off my hands and the leaf disappeared and the trees spun around and the cement flame flew over like a great bird and I was in the air and then on my back at the bottom of the steps.

At the top I could see shoes and pants and hands hanging and a red floppy face and lips snarling.

"You jackass! Out of bounds! You bums will follow the rules around here! Right from the start! Out of bounds! Jackass!"

It was the vice-principal.

A while later, everybody went into the school.

After a few speeches in the auditorium and some Home Room teacher business, some older students came around and told us about some of the clubs we could join. And some of the teams we could try out for. One team I was interested in was the gymnastics team. Then a very handsome senior student came in and told us he was president of the Boys' Hi-Y. He had on beautiful clothes and his smile was happy and his teeth were white and even. He invited anyone who was interested to join his Hi-Y Club. A very special club.

After they gave us our lockers and we signed some forms we went down to the cafeteria and got our books issued to us. While they were issuing the books the teacher in charge read out a list of names of people who hadn't paid their class fees. Those people had to get out of line and wait until the end.

There were two names on the list.

Denny Dingle, the boy we walked to school with.

And Hulbert O'Driscoll.

We didn't know anything about these class fees.

While we were waiting we walked down the basement hall where our lockers were. Near my locker was a little shop that sold chocolate bars, school supplies, gym socks and stuff.

Serving behind the little counter was the handsome Hi-Y guy who had given us the talk about the special club. The sign over the counter said, "Tuck Shop."

Back in the cafeteria just about everybody was gone.

"There's a special form you fill out if you have no money to pay your fees," the teacher told us.

Denny Dingle and I signed the forms and got our books. *Junior Science for Secondary Schools*; *General Math Book I*; *Building the Canadian Nation*; *Good Health*; *Cours Premier de Français*; *Junior Guidance for Today*; *The Merchant of Venice*; *A Book of Good Stories*.

Back down around the Tuck Shop I was standing by my open locker putting my books in and I saw Mrs. O'Driscoll coming towards me down the hall with a mop and a pail. The pail was on wheels and the mop was stuck in it and she was pushing the pail along like it was a funny-looking round dog on a wooden leash. She had on a light blue charlady's dress, with wet stains on it, rubber gloves and a rag tied around her hair. There were two boys walking behind her, imitating her.

I was going to step out from behind my locker door and talk to her, but suddenly I didn't.

Instead, I slipped along the lockers to where the Tuck Shop was, and I leaned over the little counter pretending to ask the price of some pencil sets and math sets there. When I was sure she had gone by I went back and closed my locker.

The first day of school was very short and by noon we were finished and I met Fleurette outside.

We decided to show each other our new schools. Fleurette's school and my school were attached. They didn't look attached though. They looked like one huge building. I showed Fleurette the big wide steps and the wide cement railings that were big enough to put statues on. I told her what had happened about the handstand and how the vice-principal pushed me down the stairs.

"Why did he do that?" she said. She had her eyes open wide and they were turning black.

"I don't know," I said.

"He shouldn't have done that," she said, with a tight look on her face. I was sorry I told her about it because it seemed to scare her so much.

"Did he hurt you?" she said, searching my face with her eyes.

"No, it was nothing," I said. "How could he hurt me? Nobody can hurt me." Then I showed her the shield and the torch and the words carved underneath and then we went in one of the six heavy doors tall enough to fit giants, and inside the doors the smooth, wide marble steps and the gold railings going up to the huge lobby outside the assembly hall, with the curved ceilings carved and coming down like cement cloth to the tall fat pillars.

"Are you sure he didn't hurt you?" Fleurette said. She didn't seem to be paying much attention to what I was showing her.

Leaning against one of the pillars was a tall boy by himself who was watching us.

I showed Fleurette the two shields carved in iron on the wall with the names of all the students from Glebe Collegiate Institute who were dead because of the First World War and the Second World War. I looked back at the pillar and the boy was gone. I showed Fleurette the oak case with the glass top with the holy-looking book open in there, with the wide purple ribbon bookmark in it and the fancy lists of the names of the dead with the capital letters drawn with gargoyles and animals and vines and flowers and cherubs and angels peeking out. I wondered what it would be like to have your name in that book for everybody to see.

"Wouldn't you have to be dead first?" Fleurette said.

I felt like somebody was watching us. I looked over and the tall boy was behind another one of the pillars, peeking around. He was very skinny and had flat black hair with grease on it. His ears stuck out quite a bit and his face was long and pointed like a fox.

"Wouldn't you have to be dead first?" Fleurette said again.

"Let's go over to your school," I said.

"Why?" she said, "there's nothing to see there."

"I want to. Come on," I said.

We walked up the long block to the entrance of the High School of Commerce. It had ordinary doors, ordinary steps, small cement railings that maybe one person could sit on. Inside, there was a little sign carved in the wall saying when the school opened.

While we were reading the wall the guy with a face like a fox came up behind us and pretended to read it too. He had skinny arms with black hair on them and bony hands with long fingernails. His eyebrows were black and really thick and they joined in the middle over his nose.

Then we left and walked down to Ottawa South to get the Uplands bus. Denny Dingle was there.

Fleurette Featherstone Fitchell was telling Denny and me about how nice it was at the High School of Commerce and how everybody was excited about meeting everybody and about how pleasant and kind all the teachers were.

I told her how rotten I felt when they made us get out of line and sign a special paper before we got our books. Denny just laughed and pulled fifty cents out of his pocket.

"If they want to pay for us, let them pay," he said. Then he asked us if we wanted to get off at Kelly's Inn near the sandpits and he'd treat us. The way he talked he didn't seem to care about what they thought about him at the school.

We got off the bus and went into Kelly's Inn on the highway and Denny bought us a bottle of Kik and some chips with ketchup and vinegar and lots of salt.

While Denny was lashing more salt on his chips he asked us if we wanted to go over to his place down the road. We could meet his whole family, especially his sister. His sister was twenty years old and was married to a guy and had a baby who was not even one year old. Denny was saying he was trying to teach the baby to say "Uncle Denny." It was hard to believe that Denny was somebody's uncle.

How could somebody who was so skinny and who had so many pimples be somebody's uncle?

His house was in some trees in a gully and looked like it would fall down if you touched it. "We're not rich enough to live in Uplands Emergency Shelter," he said, laughing.

When we went in they were all sitting around the room sipping lemonade. Out the window you could see the sandpits in the distance.

Denny introduced me first to the baby who was asleep in a basket. "This is the baby," he said. "She is no year's old and her name is Doris." The baby had almost no hair and one of her little fists was stuck up in the air.

"And this is the baby's mother," said Denny. "She's twenty years old and her name is Doris." Doris looked just like Denny only she wasn't skinny and she didn't have any pimples and she was beautiful.

"And this is the baby's grandmother. She's forty years old and *her* name is Doris." This Doris looked just like the last Doris except her face was a little fatter and her hair was starting to go gray. She looked pretty proud of her son Denny — of how smooth an introducer he was.

"And this is the baby's great-grandmother. She's sixty years old and guess what? *Her* name is Doris." Doris had gray hair and was knitting. She made a sweet smile.

"And this is the baby's great-*great*-grandmother. She is eighty years old and her name is, of course, *Doris!*" Doris was rocking and sipping lemonade. Her hair was snow white. She laughed. She was enjoying the introductions.

"And *this* is the baby's great-great-*great*-grandmother. She is one hundred years old and she's the greatest Doris of them all!"

The oldest Doris was humped over in a little chair in the corner with a blanket around her, sipping her lemonade through a straw. She nodded at me. She

47

had hardly any hair at all. She stuck her hard little fist in the air as if she had just won a big boxing match.

We all had some lemonade and then the baby woke up and Denny tried to make little Doris say "Uncle Denny" a few times but she wouldn't. She just smiled and blew some bubbles at him, and then we left.

We left all the Dorises and their lemonade and walked home past the Golf Club and the airplane runways to Building Number Eight, where we were richer than Denny and all the Dorises. Fleurette Featherstone Fitchell and I talked and laughed about how funny Denny and all the Dorises were, but Fleurette didn't know I was doing two things at once. I was laughing, but inside I felt sad and scared.

Sad and scared because of what I did to Mrs. O'Driscoll near my locker that day.

Outside Fleurette's door I said good-bye to her and sort of hung around to see if she'd invite me in.

She always seemed different when she was around her door. She opened it and slipped in so that I couldn't see anything. But for just a second I saw her mother at the kitchen table with her head down on her arms.

7
Job!

In science, the guy sitting beside me at my table was the skinny guy with the black flat hair and the one eyebrow who was spying on Fleurette and me the day before. He told me that he was getting some special grade nine guys to join a club called the Junior Boys' Hi-Y. He said it was a very special club. He said that his older brother was the president of the Senior Boys' Hi-Y and that someday *he* would take his brother's place and be the president. His name was Doug. Then he asked me who the girl was I was hanging around with. What was her name? Was she my girlfriend? Then he showed me some other guys around the room who he might get into the special club.

"It's a very special club," he said. "And it's hard to get into. People who get into it become successes in later life," he said. "I could maybe get you in if you wanted." I was trying to figure out why he was being so nice to me.

In fact, I was trying to figure out almost everything about school.

It all seemed pretty confusing. In history we were studying our book, *Building the Canadian Nation*. Our history teacher read out how Henry Hudson was put in a little boat with his son and how the mutineers pushed the little rowboat out into the icy water and how they sailed away, and how Henry Hudson and his son were never seen again.

And all the way home on the Uplands bus I kept thinking about what Henry Hudson and his son talked about as they rowed and floated along looking for shore and hoping they'd maybe find a way to live somehow in the cold in Canada.

Denny Dingle told me to quit worrying about it.

Fleurette said she thought it was nice that I would worry about something like that.

And I kept thinking about how awful it would have been if they didn't say anything to each other. But that couldn't be. They must have said stuff to each other. They must have given up rowing after a while and the father must have asked the son if he was cold and if he wanted a drink of water and the son must have come up to the middle seat in the boat and sat inside the father's coat to keep warm. There was a picture of them in the book.

And they must have gone to sleep that way.

Saying things to each other.

Denny kept getting A's on his tests. I was getting D's and F's.

"All you have to do is remember the dates," Denny said, "never mind that other stuff."

And in history the teacher made us read about Canada and its native peoples.

He told us that the native Canadians had no animals except dogs. There were no horses, cows, pigs or sheep. The white man brought all those animals over with him and gave them to the Indians.

"They had animals," Denny said, "but they were all wild. It's common sense."

We read in the book how the Canadian Indians lived from hand to mouth and from place to place. And how some other Indians lived in a "longhouse" the book said. The longhouse was made of a wood frame covered with bark, and was divided on each side into several cubicles, each occupied by a family, while down the centre ran a common passageway in which the fires were built.

It was sort of like where I lived except for the bark and the fires.

Another A for Denny and an F for me.

And the Hi-Y guys all laughed when the teacher made us read in the book how the Indians never invented the wheel. Everybody else had the wheel. Everybody except the caveman. And he was pretty well just a monkey.

And then we tried to have a discussion.

"And now we'll have a discussion about that," the teacher said.

And a Hi-Y guy got up and said that he thought that because the Indians didn't invent the wheel they were the stupidest people on the planet Earth. They were very unsuccessful.

"And what do you have to say about that, Lawrence?" the teacher said to Broken Arrow, an Indian kid who sat at the back who was from Maniwaki with his big dark face.

"They had water and canoes. They didn't need wheels," said Broken Arrow.

And all the Hi-Y guys and the Welfare Club girls laughed and giggled and whispered things about Broken Arrow and the teacher stamped his foot and said that will be enough of that.

And the discussion was over.

That's the way all the history discussions wound up.

"That will be enough of that!"

And I kept wondering how these guys got to be Hi-Y guys so fast. They were new at the school, just like I was.

And Denny Dingle just laughed and told me to quit worrying about it.

We weren't allowed to go over to the Commerce side of the school between classes or at lunchtime so at noon I'd eat my lunch fast just standing around my locker and around the Tuck Shop and then I'd go down to the corner of Bronson and Carling and meet Fleurette and we'd walk around the block together a few times until the bell rang.

And in guidance we had a guidance book where there were a whole lot of questions and answers with little drawings beside them. One question was about applying for a job. It asked if you would apply for a job this way (a) or this way (b). Under (a) there was a picture of a guy applying for a job sitting in a chair in front of some big shot's desk. The big shot was there with his two phones and his pen set and his photograph of his family and his face, very interested, looking at the younger guy in the chair. The younger guy who was applying for the job was sitting up very straight with his legs crossed and his hands folded in his lap and his pants all pressed just like knives and his shoes shining with little windows of shininess in each one and his tie up nice and neat and straight and his suit jacket buttoned and his hair all slicked back and a big smile on him, but somebody had inked in his teeth and crossed his eyes. He looked like the guy who ran the Tuck Shop except for the inked-in part.

Under (b) it showed the same big shot at the same desk but this time with a really disgusted look on his face like he had just swallowed a piece of rotten fish or something. The younger guy who was applying for the job wasn't in the other chair, he was sitting on the big shot's desk. He had pushed over the pen set and the family picture to make room for himself and he was leaning over breathing in the big shot's face. His hair was all knotted and ratty and his face was dirty-looking and there was spray coming out between his scummy-looking teeth. He had on a tight T-shirt and you could see the hair sticking out from under his arms. His pants were filthy and the bottoms were in rags and his shoes were turned up at the toes and scuffed and untied. There were mud marks on the floor where he had walked in mud or something worse. There were little squiggly lines coming up from each footprint.

Was the answer (a) or (b)?

These were the kind of questions we got to answer in our guidance book.

You were supposed to pick which was the best way to apply for a job. Very confusing. Did this have something to do with why I didn't get all those jobs I applied for?

And most days after school I'd meet Fleurette and Denny and we'd walk down to the Uplands bus and talk and laugh about school. And Fleurette would try to help me figure out some of these confusing things about school and some of the subjects we took.

The thing I didn't tell them was this: that there was one thing I had figured out perfectly about school, and that was how not to see, ever to see, Mrs. O'Driscoll. I knew exactly where she'd be every minute of the day, and I was always somewhere else.

And in science we always seemed to be taking the grasshopper.

The Hi-Y guys had more fun there than anywhere.

One day they had a bushel basket of leaves tied out the window. Every time Mr. Tool, our science teacher, turned around to draw another tibia or a mandible on the grasshopper one of the Hi-Y guys closest to the window jumped up and grabbed a handful of leaves out of the basket and fired them up in the air over the class and then sat down and buried his head in his grasshopper drawing. Mr. Tool turned around again just in time to see the last few leaves falling.

"Where are those leaves coming from?" Mr. Tool asked.

"Probably blew in the window," the Hi-Y guys said.

"How can they blow in the third floor window, boys? Leaves don't fly around at this altitude."

"Must have been a hurricane or something," the Hi-Y guys said.

While all this was going on I had a little chat with Doug, the big shot in the Junior Hi-Y, who shared my table with me. His hand on my arm was cold and clammy and his eyebrow was moving up and down like a window blind.

"Why don't you put your name in to join the Junior Hi-Y?" said Doug.

"What *is* the Hi-Y, anyway?" I said. I wanted to hear him explain it some more.

"It's a very special club. We have meetings every Thursday night at the downtown YMCA and we organize a big dance once a year and executives get to sit on the stage sometimes to welcome important visitors to the school during assemblies. We also get trips. Last year the Senior Hi-Y went to New York City to the United Nations to encourage peace among all nations in this world of ours. The president and the vice-president get their pictures in the paper every year. Many former Hi-Y members are now big successes in the world. You have to be all-round to join. Are you all-round?"

"All-round what?" I said.

"All-round. You know. Be on a team and also get pretty good marks. And fool around a bit. Not be a goody-goody."

More leaves were floating down and Mr. Tool was looking at the ceiling to see where they were coming from.

"Here's an application form. Fill it out and I'll hand it in," said Doug. Then he said, "How's your girlfriend?"

I looked at the application form while leaves floated down to the floor.

NAME:

ADDRESS:

PHONE NUMBER:

AMBITION:

EXPERIENCE IN CLUBS:

AWARDS:

TEAMS:

FATHER'S OCCUPATION:

MAKE AND YEAR OF FATHER'S CAR:

RELIGION:

While I was looking at the application I noticed somebody at the classroom door. It was Chubby, the principal of Glebe Collegiate. He leaned in and asked Mr. Tool if there was an O'Driscoll boy in the class.

I went to the door and out into the hall and Chubby, who was puffing deep and hard, told me about a job that I could have. I wondered how he would even know my name. Chubby was a fat man with a wrinkly suit that seemed too small for him and he leaned hard on a cane. So hard that his knuckles were white.

"I have a part-time job for you O'Driscoll, if you want it. Two nights a week. You stay overnight at an elderly lady's house so she won't be alone. That's the two nights her nurse takes a holiday. Tuesday and Thursday. Every Tuesday and Thursday you go over after school and sleep over. She's old and sick.

She needs somebody with her. She gets scared by herself."

"Why do I get to get the job?" I said to Chubby, hoping he'd get his breath.

Chubby looked right in my eyes and puffed a few times. Then his voice changed a little bit and he said, "I picked your name out of a hat."

For a minute I had a funny feeling that he was lying. Then I forgot about it.

"You get five dollars a night. She'll give it to you each morning before you leave."

Five dollars!

After he gave me the lady's name and the address I went back in the room and sat down and looked at it.

Miss L. Collar-Cuff,
210 Easy Avenue, Ottawa.

It was about two blocks from the school.

One of the richest streets in Ottawa.

Leaves were floating down in the room and Doug was squatting on our table pretending he was a grasshopper.

After school that day I tried out for the gym team. It was quite late when I got to the bus and for the first time I went home without Fleurette or Denny.

I sat in the empty seat beside one of my neighbours, Mr. Yasso.

Everybody called him that because that's just about all he ever said. If you met him in the hall or in the lineup for the toilet and you said, "Nice day," he'd say "Yeah, so?"

Mr. Yasso was a garbageman in Ottawa.

On the Uplands bus at night nobody wanted to sit with him because he was such a rotten conversationalist. And also he smelled like he had garbage in all of his pockets.

Mrs. O'Driscoll didn't like him. She would maybe be out in the hall at the tubs doing a washing and Mr. Yasso would be standing there. He often stood around there, leaning against the tubs or against the wall or looking out the window at the boy with no brain sitting out there.

"That poor child just sits there, day after day," Mrs. O'Driscoll might say, trying to make conversation.

"Yeah, so?" Mr. Yasso would say.

"Why does Mr. Yasso stand around out in the hall so much?" I said one time to Mrs. O'Driscoll. "He seems to be out there all the time."

"He's out there because he likes to talk to everybody. He's such a wonderful conversationalist," Mrs. O'Driscoll said out of the corner of her mouth. "He drives me crazy!"

"Yeah, so?" I said, making a little joke.

I sat down beside him on the bus.

He smelled pretty awful, but I tried to start a conversation with him because, after all, he lived in the same building I did. A conversation is two people speaking to each other. You take turns listening to the other person. You try to help the other person out so that you can each say things back and forward for a while. That way you can find out about each other, learn some things, maybe even have some fun.

On the bus I tried to start a conversation with Mr. Yasso.

"I'm coming home pretty late today because I'm trying out for the gym team at school," I said.

"Yeah, so?" said Mr. Yasso.

Although I was dying to tell somebody about my new job with Miss Collar-Cuff on Easy Avenue, I didn't bother even trying with Mr. Yasso.

8
Light the Light

Just as I got in the back door of our building I saw a big man with red hair leaving Fleurette's place. He closed the door quietly. Then the hall was empty. At the other end there was a horrible noise coming from behind Mrs. Quirk's door where she lived with the boy with no brain. A sound I'd never heard from there before. A sort of snoring. I put my hand on her door to feel the vibrations. The door wasn't shaking but I could feel it trembling as I rested my hand lightly on it.

Fleurette was at our place and Mrs. O'Driscoll told us all about it as I looked in the pot she had on the stove. She was boiling some chicken and potatoes. I would wait until we sat down to eat to tell her about my job.

"Mrs. Quirk moved out late last night. Her poor child went into a kind of a coma and some people came in a truck and took her and her child and her stuff away in the quiet of the night. Mrs. Blank told me all about it today when I got home from work. And about an hour later, no more, no less, another family moved in. A wife and her man. Mr. and Mrs. Stentorian. That's him you hear snoring out there. They were living in a tent, can you imagine, waiting for a vacancy out here! And it being November! That poor woman. Listen to that! If O'Driscoll could only hear that. You know, I don't think he's drowned at all. He's out there somewhere! I wonder what he'd say about this man Stentorian and his snoring!"

She was piling chicken and potatoes on a plate for me. And talking away. Fleurette said she had to go and I went out in the hall with her and asked her who the man was who was at her place.

"I don't know," she said, and walked down the hall to her door.

When I went back in, Mrs. O'Driscoll was still talking.

"And Mrs. Blank told me that Mrs. Stentorian told her that in that tent where they were living he snored so bad one night that some of the people in the other tents around got together and called the police. Can you imagine? Calling the police for snoring. Isn't that a good one? O'Driscoll would like that one!" She was using the corner of her mouth when she mentioned O'Driscoll.

While I was eating, I told Mrs. O'Driscoll about my new job minding Miss Collar-Cuff on Easy Avenue.

"That's one fancy street, Hubbo, my boy," said Mrs. O'Driscoll. "Isn't that grand now! A job on Easy Avenue! Well, you'll do well by her. You're a nice boy and you're a thoughtful boy. Every Tuesday and Thursday is it? That's tomorrow! You'll have to have a set of pajamas or a nightshirt or something for going to bed. I know! I've got the very thing! One of O'Driscoll's nightshirts. I didn't have the heart to throw it out. I'll cut some off the bottom and hem it up and wash and starch it for you. You'll be slick as a button!"

While I finished the chicken and potatoes, Mrs. O'Driscoll got out the nightshirt and the scissors and the needle and thread.

"Now this job you got calls for a celebration. I've got a nice surprise for you. Chubby gave us all a nice gift today with our pay cheques because we did such a good job keeping his school clean for him. He's a grand man, so thoughtful and kind. And him with that pain that he's always in. My gift was this beautiful bottle of sherry!"

Mrs. O'Driscoll got out two glasses, one for me and one for her, and poured us each some sherry.

"Now I'd imagine, I might be wrong, but I'd imagine this is the first time you've ever had a drink of anything like this. Taste it. You'll like it. And here's to your new job. Imagine! Easy Avenue! Won't you be the fancy one every Tuesday and Thursday!"

I sipped the sherry. It was sweet and warm down my throat.

Mrs. O'Driscoll took a gulp of hers and sang a little song that she sometimes sang.

Pack up all my care and woe.
Here I go, singin' low.
Bye, bye, blackbird!
Where somebody waits for me,
Sugar's sweet, so is she.
Bye, bye, blackbird!
No one here can love and understand me.
Oh what hard luck stories they all hand me.
Make my bed, light the light.
I'll arrive, late tonight.
Black Birrrrd,
Bye, bye!

Then she wiped her eyes with O'Driscoll's nightshirt.

"O'Driscoll and I would sing that whenever we'd have a little nip together. Oh, he was a nice fella. I don't think he's drowned at all, you know!"

Mrs. O'Driscoll poured some more sherry.

While she was cutting off the nightshirt I started telling her about school and Chubby and the Hi-Y boys and how confusing some of my subjects were and guidance and science and history.

"It's grand that you're going to a fine school, my boy. Learning all those things about history and science will make you happy in the long run, no question about it! And that Chubby, what a grand man he is. I'm sure he's the one got you that job over on Easy Avenue. He had a long chat with me when I first went there to work in the summer. He knew you'd appreciate his help. He knows all about O'Driscoll and you and your parents and where we live and everything about us. What a grand man. I'm sure he's the one!

Pack up all my care and woe.
Here I go,
singing low.
Bye, bye, Blackbird!

"Tell me some more about school, Hubbo, my boy!"

Mrs. O'Driscoll poured some more sherry.

I told her all about our English class and how we were reading a story in our *Book of Good Stories* called "How Much Land Does A Man Need?" by Leo Tolstoy. In the story a man is offered, for a cheap price, all the land that he can circle around on foot in one day. He can leave at sunrise and go as far as he likes in a big circle and when he comes back to the same spot at sunset, all the land he has walked around will be his. If he doesn't get back by sunset he'll lose his deposit. Of course, the man wants so much that he starts running and although he gets back at sunset just in time, he is so exhausted he dies. So they bury him right there and that's all the land he needs. Six feet for his grave.

"Ain't it the truth!" said Mrs. O'Driscoll, and banged the table.

"I've read that story and I've read other stuff by Leo Tolstoy — a great, wise man he was! Do you remember in the story, the blood that came out of his mouth just before he died? That's a little more than exhausted."

"The teacher said 'exhausted'," I said quietly, but I guess I had a surprised look on my face because I never thought Mrs. O'Driscoll ever read any books.

"You're surprised that Mrs. O'Driscoll, only a cleaning lady, can read a book now and then, Hubbo, my boy! That's a grand writer! Wait till you read *War and Peace*! There's lots to happen yet for you and Leo Tolstoy! Don't worry your head about it. You didn't hurt my feelings. Here, give us a hug. That's it. Now, have some more sherry! Yes, a grand story!"

I was feeling a little bit dizzy because of the sherry.

Did she know how I was avoiding her at school?

"Oh, Hubbo," said Mrs. O'Driscoll, "life is so lovely!"

She was trying to thread her needle to hem up O'Driscoll's nightshirt for me.

Did she know what a traitor I was?

"And so short! Life I mean. Not the nightshirt!" Then she let out a big laugh.

Did she know what a sneaky rat I was?

"I'll do this in the morning," she said, putting down the needle and thread and pouring some more sherry for herself.

Later on, in bed, I could hear, over the wall, Mrs. O'Driscoll in her room, laughing a bit, then crying some, then snoring a little bit.

And then I went spinning to sleep.

9
Easy Avenue

Thursday after gymnastics, at about 5:30, I climbed the wide front steps up to the huge curved verandah at 210 Easy Avenue for my first day on the job. The door was heavy and black and the knocker was shiny brass. Miss Collar-Cuff's nurse opened the door and introduced herself and brought me into the dining room while she put on her coat. There was a huge table there, set for one.

"See you next Tuesday," she said, "if you work out." Then she touched me on the arm and left.

Miss Collar-Cuff was sitting in a big plush chair in her living room beside the fireplace that had tall gold lions on each side guarding the fire. The reflection of the flames was flickering in the glass eyes of the lions, making them look like they were blinking.

I sat at the dining-room table and a lady dressed as a cook brought my supper to me. It was three fat, sizzling pork chops with mint sauce and potatoes and tiny carrots that looked like candies. I tried to move my plate a bit but I burnt my fingers.

"Don't touch the plate," said the lady. "It's hot."

And all the milk you wanted. And hot apple pie with cheese on it.

The napkin beside my plate was made of heavy white cloth and was rolled up in a silver ring. The ring and the napkin had fancy engraved letters on them. C.C.

Three glasses of milk. And the glass seemed just as heavy when it was empty as it did when it was full. The table was long and shiny and black. The salt and pepper shakers were tall silver statues of a king and queen.

After I finished eating the supper I took my dishes into the kitchen and the lady dressed as a cook in there told me I didn't have to do that anymore.

"Don't forget," she said, "when you come back on Tuesday, you leave the dishes right where they are. That's if you're back on Tuesday."

I went into the living room and sat down on the chesterfield and looked at Miss Collar-Cuff and the blinking lions. She was very thin and her skin looked like white silk. She had on a long black dress with white frills around her wrists and around her throat. She sat very straight and very stiff, and with her chin up she looked like she was looking down her own long face and then at me.

She sat so still, staring at me, that I had to look away. I looked down at my legs and then at my raggedy shoes, then over to the window, then down at the flowered pattern of the couch, then at some paintings on the wall. Then at the blinking lions. Then back at her.

The lions seemed to move around more than she did.

I was wondering what Nerves would do if he were sitting here. I put my head back and looked down my face at her the way Nerves might but I knew I couldn't last. I would have a better chance of winning a staring contest with one of the lions.

Suddenly she broke the spell.

"Are you a nice boy?" she said.

A nice boy. I didn't know what to say. What was a nice boy? What did she want to hear? What would Mrs. O'Driscoll say? She would just start talking. Say anything. Let the words fall out all over the couch and the rug and fill up the room until you were up to your knees in words about this and that and the other thing. Or what would Fleurette Featherstone Fitchell say? She'd probably pause, think about it, and then say *one* word. Yes, for instance. Just yes.

I tried a Fleurette answer.

"Yes," I said.

Miss Collar-Cuff seemed pleased with this. She waited for a long time while I watched the lions blinking away. Then she asked me another one.

"Are you handsome?" she asked.

Was I handsome? I almost got up and walked over to one of the mirrors in the hallway to look at myself. To get the answer. But I was glad I didn't. She probably would have thought I was just trying to be clever or something. Mrs. O'Driscoll once told me I was handsome but not to worry about it. I'd get over it soon enough, she said. Mr. O'Driscoll was handsome, she said. But he *never* got over it. Probably out there now somewhere, looking at himself in a mirror in some foreign country, she said.

"Mrs. O'Driscoll said I was handsome once, but that I'd get over it," I said.

"Mrs. O'Driscoll?"

"She's sort of my mother."

"I see," she said. She was smiling a little bit.

"And are you popular?"

This was getting to be about the worst conversation I ever had in my life. My mind was a blank. I felt like the boy with no brain. Sitting there empty. Then I felt my mouth stretch over like Mrs. O'Driscoll's did sometimes when she was being specially sarcastic. Out of the corner of my mouth came the answer. I could hardly believe it was me. I think even the lions were surprised.

"Well, people aren't exactly stopping me on the street to ask for my autograph." I even *sounded* like Mrs. O'Driscoll.

"Oh, witty," said Miss Collar-Cuff. "And are you intelligent in school?"

"Yes," I said. I was ready to tell her anything.

"And are you a good athlete?"

"Yes. Would you like me to show you a trick?" I was desperate.

I jumped up and went into the kitchen. The lady, who was now not dressed as a cook, was leaving by the back door. I brought out a wooden chair and set it on the deep rug in the middle of the living room.

I sat in the chair. I put one hand on the back of the chair and the other on the seat between my legs. Then I leaned forward and pressed up into a perfect handstand. I could hold it for as long as she wanted. I could have stayed there for an hour. I was locked in perfect position. I took a quick peek at her. Her eyes were shining with excitement. At least this way, I didn't have to talk.

Suddenly she started slapping her thin little hands together, giving me a big round of applause. Then I came down slowly to show how much control I had.

While I was in the kitchen putting the chair back she called to me.

"What book are you reading in school?"

"*A Book of Good Stories*," I said.

"What story?" she said when I was back in the living room feeling the lions' glass eyes.

"How Much Land Does a Man Need?" I told her.

"Ah, Tolstoy," she said. "Go in the den and you'll find everthing Tolstoy ever wrote under T. Bring a

big book called *War and Peace Part One* to me."
The den was lined with books to the ceiling. They
were in alphabetical order and when I got to the T's
there was half a shelf full of Leo Tolstoy. I got down
the one called *War and Peace Part One* while I
thought of what Mrs. O'Driscoll would have to say
about this. The cover was black velvet and the let-
tering gold. The pages were thin and silky and the
edges were dipped in silver.

"Have you read *War and Peace*?" asked Miss
Collar-Cuff.

I gave her a Fleurette Featherstone Fitchell no.

"Then you may read it to me."

And so I sat down between the blinking lions by
the fire and began to read.

"*Eh bien, mon prince*, so Genoa and Lucca are
now no more than private estates of the Bonaparte
family . . ." is the way the book starts.

Miss Collar-Cuff closed her eyes and sighed.

Later, in O'Driscoll's nightshirt, I was in the biggest bed in the world. There was room for just about
everybody in Building Number Eight in there. Mr.
and Mrs. Blank, Nerves, Mr. and Mrs. Stentorian,
Mrs. Quirk and the boy with no brain, Mr. Yasso
and Fleurette. Everybody. Put Chubby in there
too. And Denny Dingle and all the Dorises if they
wanted. And the Hi-Y guys. And Mrs. O'Driscoll.
And O'Driscoll who was supposed to be drowned.
And Fleurette's mother. And the man with the black
hair. And the man with the red hair too.

Now and then the lights of a car passed evenly
over the ceiling, and the bed lit up a bit, and I could
see the lump in the covers about half way down
where my feet were pointing up. And I felt the silk
of the comforter with my hands and pushed my head
just a little into the feathers of the pillow.

And the light sometimes glittered off the gold doorknob of the door and the silver candlesticks in front of the mirror and the shiny brass posts of the bed and the copper statues of angels and eagles and the glittering mirrors.

And the oak and mahogany furniture sat there solid and heavy and quiet.

And sleep tried to come.

Sleep tried to come quietly and silently slipping over me so I could slide down the long slide of sleep.

Suddenly my eyes clicked open and I saw that the end of the bed was shaped differently in the dark. There was a shape between the posts. A person was standing there.

A car went by and the light passed evenly over the ceiling and flashed off the gold and the silver and the brass and the copper and for a second over the face of Miss Collar-Cuff. And off the tears on her cheeks.

"It's all right," she said, standing there. "It's all right. I'll go away in a minute. I just wanted to watch you sleeping. May I watch you sleeping?"

I closed my eyes and waited.

And then sleep came.

What a job.

A lot better than the Cinderella Book Store.

10
Success

Doug had his bony, hairy arms across my note-book in science class. His greasy hair was stuck right near my face and he was making me sick. Also making me sick was the smell of the stink perfume some of the Hi-Y guys were pouring on Mr. Tool's stuffed owl.

Doug leaned over because he saw me filling out part of the Hi-Y application form. I had put next to the word ADDRESS, the words 210 Easy Avenue. When I saw that he saw me, I tucked the form into my science notebook with all the pictures of the grasshopper. Then he put his bony, hairy arms across my book.

"Haven't you got that thing filled out yet?" he said. "Do you ever take your girlfriend Fleurette anywhere? Where does she live? What do you do when you take her somewhere?"

"None of your business, Doug," I said.

"Is she dirty?" Doug said. His eyebrow was moving up and down.

"Doug, get your arms off of my notebook!" I said. I was going to say, "or I'll punch your ugly face off!" but I didn't. I guess I didn't because I wanted to be in the Hi-Y and be a success. And Doug could get me in.

After school while we were waiting for the Up-lands bus I told Fleurette all about my job with Miss Collar-Cuff—the lions and *War and Peace* and my sort of dream in the big bed and how she came in the room to watch me sleep.

"Oh, Hubbo," she said, "you're so good at things. Someday you're going to be somebody. You're going to be a big success."

On the bus we were snuggled up and I asked her if she wanted to go to the Mayfair Theatre on Sat-urday to see the movie *The Jolson Story*. I could pay our way.

At home, when I told Mrs. O'Driscoll about Miss Collar-Cuff crying beside the bed she shook her head and looked very sad.

"Poor thing," she said, "all that money and so lonely and unhappy. Isn't it awful? I wonder what O'Driscoll would say? I don't know what he'd maybe say but I know what he'd probably do. He'd prob-ably move in with her as a handyman or something and then get her to give him her chequebook and help her spend all her money and get her to put him in her will and inherit every cent she's got and the house and the car . . . and that's probably what he's doing right now, sweet talking some rich old lady out of her vast fortune on some fancy ranch somewhere with oil wells and gold mines . . ."

On Saturday at the Mayfair Theatre during *The Jolson Story* Fleurette started to cry when they sang the Anniversary Waltz about his parents who were married for such a long time and who were so happy and who loved each other. Then she said that I was really lucky because Mrs. O'Driscoll loved me so much and always thought of me and was always nice to me and did things for me all the time and hugged me all the time. She put her head on my shoulder and I started asking her about her family, and I asked

71

her who the man with the black hair and dark eyes was and she said that he was her father and that he was very kind and that he had to travel around all the time because of his job but he always came home whenever he could and brought her and her mother gifts and loved them very much, and how he was a wonderful man. I tried to see her face when she was saying these things but I couldn't because her chin was tucked in my neck. I asked her who the man with the red hair was and she told me that he was her uncle and that he would come over sometimes and bring gifts and see how they were and that he was kind and very funny and would tell them funny stories of things that happened to him in his travels. And her voice sounded different when she was telling all this and I tried to see her face but I couldn't.

We were talking so much that the people behind us told us to shut up and if we wanted to argue we should go somewhere else. Funny how sometimes when you are talking about private things people think you are arguing.

After the show we saw the handsome Hi-Y guy who ran the Tuck Shop. He was with his girlfriend with the fancy clothes. I said hello to them as they passed by but they didn't answer me.

"Do you know them?" Fleurette asked. "What are you saying hello to them for if you don't even know them?"

I didn't know what to tell her.

A few weeks later I had guidance again and Mr. Stubbs was telling us all about success.

He mumbled quite a bit and looked up at the ceiling and out the window and at his shoes a lot. He would start saying something about how to be a big success and then he'd mumble lower and lower until you could hardly hear him and then he'd be looking out the window and up at the sky and although his lips would still be moving there would be no sound coming out and all the kids would be saying "There he goes again," and "Good-bye Mr. Stubbs," and singing bits of songs like "Dream" and "Rock-a-bye Baby."

Then he would seem to wake up and look around the room at the blackboard and at his desk and at the students and at the door and at all the pictures on the walls of big successes like Napoleon and Prime Minister King and Shakespeare and Lassie, the famous movie star dog, and everbody. It seemed like he had just landed there from somewhere else, some other planet maybe, and was trying to figure out where he was. His shirt was always wrinkled and dirty-looking and his tie was tied so that the thin part was longer than the wide part and the shoulders of his suit were quite lumpy, as though there were golf balls or something stuffed in the lining. His fly was usually open part way, and there was always egg or soup or something on his pants.

He didn't look very successful.

Then when he found out where he was he'd walk over to another part of the room and try again, telling us about how to be a big success in life.

And the kids would be saying stuff like "He's back," or "He's okay," and singing parts of songs like "Hello, Everybody, Hello!" or "When the Lights Go On Again."

This day we had a test.

He gave everybody a little piece of paper and told us to open our guidance books.

There were two drawings.

One was a picture of a doctor in a nice white lab coat. He was holding a clipboard and he had a stethoscope around his neck and a round metal disk on his forehead. He was very handsome and was smiling with a row of perfect teeth at a beautiful lady who was lying in a bed and smiling right back at him. Her hair was done up like she was all better and would hop right out of bed any minute now and go right to the dance with the handsome doctor.

Beside it was a drawing of a garbageman carrying a big pail of stinking garbage over to a truck with another guy in the back standing there waiting to catch the pail up to his waist in garbage. The guy carrying the pail was bent over a bit with lines showing how sore his back was. There were flies swarming around his head and sitting on his lips.

There was a question under the two drawings: "Which would you rather be? A or B?"

The test wasn't too hard. We had to write down A or B on the little piece of paper and sign our name on it and hand it in.

A was for the doctor.

B was for the garbageman.

As a joke I put down B and signed my name and handed it in.

While we were reading a little story in our book about a crippled orphan who became a billionaire somehow, Mr. Stubbs was going over the pieces of paper we handed in. I saw him put one piece of paper aside. It turned out to be mine.

At the end of the class while everybody was crammed in the doorway and trampling on each other trying to get out, I heard the name O'Driscoll.

I stopped at his desk to see if I heard what I heard.

"Come after school so that we can have a guidance chat," Mr. Stubbs said.

"But I have to go to gymnastics practice," I said.

"It's compulsory," he said. "You failed your test. You said B, O'Driscoll. The answer is A. A for doctor."

"But I just did it as a joke," I said.

"No you didn't."

"No, really. I want to be a doctor. I only said garbageman as a kind of joke. For a bit of a laugh."

"Not funny. After school."

"I could change it. I could put A down. I want to be a doctor worse than anything. It's been my life-long ambition since I was about six months old to be a doctor. And not just an ordinary doctor. A brain surgeon. I want to cure everybody in Canada and be famous and rich and get the Nobel Prize for doctoring and have a statue of me in the park. And start my own hospital . . ."

It was no use.

Mr. Stubbs was already looking out the window again. His eyes were fogging over fast. He was gone on a long one this time.

Later that day I found out that just about everybody in the class had put down B for garbageman.

After school Mr. Stubbs and I started all over again.

"You put down B for garbageman," he said.

"But I only did it as a joke. I don't want to be a garbageman." I looked at the clock. The gym team was already warming up. Tonight after practice the coach would put up the list of the eight guys who would make the team. Four seniors and four juniors.

"What about all the others who put down B for garbageman?" I said. "What about them?"

"They were only fooling," he said. "Making a joke."

"So was I," I said.

"No you weren't," he said. He had his jacket buttoned wrong. He looked like he was going to fall apart.

"You see, I know where you come from. You come from Uplands Emergency Shelter. You people have got to think about your future. You've got to be more ambitious. Look at these pictures on the wall here.

You could be like Shakespeare or Prime Minister King or Napoleon. Or Lassie."

"Lassie's a dog," I said, but he didn't hear me.

He was off on his success speech. I waited until he really got rolling about success, and sure enough, he started mumbling and murmuring and his eyes rolled up and he was looking out the window up at the sky and mumbling himself into a real hypnotic trance. He was heading out on a very long journey. I waited until he was really gone and then I slipped out and ran down to get changed for gymnastic practice.

After practice we all gathered around the bulletin board while the coach put up the list saying who made the team.

My name was on the list.

The next day in science class I secretly took out the Hi-Y application form.

Beside the word TEAMS I wrote "Glebe Gym Team."

Beside the word TELEPHONE I put Miss Collar-Cuff's number, and I put "Tuesdays and Thursdays only."

Beside the words MAKE AND YEAR OF FATHER'S CAR I put "Cadillac" because that's the kind of car Miss Collar-Cuff had in her locked garage.

11
Mysterious Money

Denny Dingle was first in our class in everything but English. But he was always near the top in that too because I used to explain everything to him that we read.

But suddenly something happened to him that made him come just about last in everything.

A new girl came to class.

And Denny started acting like the boy with no brain.

She had on a very frilly blouse that you could see through. She had on a tight red skirt with a slit up the side. She had on silk stockings with seams straight up the back. She had on red high-heeled shoes. She had a tiny chain around her left ankle. She had bracelets around her wrists. She had a silver tiara in her long blond straight silky hair. She had lipstick on her very curvy lips and she had long eyelashes and she had rouge on her cheeks. And a black beauty spot beside her mouth.

And big cold blue eyes.

She walked very slowly, carrying her books, her chin up, not looking at anybody.

Like a queen.

When she came in the room, she came in last. Everybody knew she would be last. She came in, walking slowly, her high heels clicking on the floor, click, click, as she walked, the little wind she made full of perfume when she went by you, the sound of her jingling bracelets as she slid into her desk, the room so silent, as if a tiger had just strolled in and sat down.

Her name was Melody Bleach.

I looked over at Denny Dingle as Melody took her seat. He had a funny look on his face.

The next day when Melody Bleach came clicking in, I watched Denny. He was looking at her, following her with his eyes. He looked like Melody had just hit him over the head with a big wet fish.

The next day when Melody Bleach came in, I watched Denny. He was watching her, his mouth hanging open, his eyes glazed over, as though he were being hypnotized by Dracula.

The next day, Denny wasn't there when Melody Bleach came in. I knew he was at school because he was on the bus with me that morning. Something was wrong. Suddenly, just as we heard Melody's bracelets jangling on her desk as she sat down, in came Denny. He had been following her. He walked in the room like a zombie. If he had been wrapped in bandages he would have been a perfect mummy. You could have snapped your fingers in front of his face and he wouldn't have noticed.

On the bus that night he sat there staring straight ahead. I felt his head to see if he had a fever. A little while later he spoke. I couldn't hear him at first because of all the noise and arguing behind us. I put my ear up to his mouth.

"I know where her locker is," is what he said.

He sounded like he just confessed to a murder.

He sounded like he said, "I just murdered my whole family."

Poor Denny. He was in bad shape.

The next day before class I followed him. He walked from his locker in the basement near the gym, up to the first floor outside the auditorium where most of our class was hanging around waiting for the assembly doors to open.

He walked by while everybody stared at him and went up to the second floor and then to the third floor, to the lockers near the art room.

Melody was standing with her locker door open, using the mirror that hung on the inside of the door. She was touching up her beauty spot with a makeup pencil.

Denny stood behind her. She raised her eyes and looked at Denny's reflection. Her eyelashes, when they came up, just about knocked the mirror off the door.

"Do you like me?" she said.

Denny's lips moved, but nothing seemed to come out. His face was the colour of ashes, which made his pimples stand out like little red lights.

"Am I pretty?" said Melody Bleach, going back to work with her pencil.

She had her tongue stuck out a bit. Some people do that when they concentrate. Suddenly I remembered her. She used to go to York Street School. She used to stick her tongue out like that when she tried to write. Her parents must have gotten rich or something, because where would she get all the fancy clothes? I remembered everybody used to say that she wet herself sitting in her seat in grade three.

"Do you think I'm pretty?" she asked Denny again.

"Yes," Denny said, tearing his eyes away from her reflection and looking down at his feet.

"Come here," said Melody, pointing to the floor beside her. "You may carry my books." On the floor her books were piled in a neat stack, the math set and the pencil box on top.

Denny picked up her books and followed her down the hall.

But that afternoon, something happened to me that took my mind off Denny. And off almost everything.

We were in English class.

Chubby came to the door while the Hi-Y guys were doing their humming song. They were all staring at their books pretending to read but humming. Whenever the teacher came down the aisle to try and find out who was doing the humming, another Hi-Y guy would start on the other side of the room.

Chubby came to the door and said something to the teacher. Then the teacher looked down at me and nodded, and then came part way down the aisle and pointed at me and told me in a sort of a whisper that the principal wanted to see me.

The Hi-Y guys hummed a little tune to go with my walk to the door.

Chubby was out in the hall leaning a lot on his cane and puffing. He said that we had to go down to the office because there was something important. I thought it was because of the humming and that I was being blamed for it.

All the way down the stairs I was planning what I would say. I was going to tell Chubby about how we were taking the same story for months now, and how I'd read it so many times I almost knew it off by heart. So that he wouldn't think I was wasting my time humming.

I thought that if I made conversation with him, got him talking while we were going downstairs, it would take his mind off the pain. He was so crippled. And there was sweat on his lip.

"What do the words *Alere* and *Flammam* mean?" I asked Chubby. *Alere* and *Flammam* were the two words written in stone on the shield over the front doors of the school.

"*Alere Flammam* is Latin," said Chubby as he struggled down each step. "It means 'Kindle the torch' or 'exalt the flame' or 'hold up the fire' . . ." We were almost at the bottom of the stairs. " . . . or 'raise the torch' or 'brandish the spark' or 'ignite the lamp' or 'elevate the ember' . . . that sort of thing."

I was glad when he stopped. All those meanings were making me dizzy.

That night I told Mrs. O'Driscoll as many of the meanings as I could remember. She said that O'Driscoll would say that none of those meanings were quite right.

"He'd have a better one than those," said Mrs. O'Driscoll. "He'd say it meant 'Light the Light!' "

After I thought about it I thought she was right. Her translation was the best one. Light the Light. It had a nice ring to it. It was also a line from her favourite song.

Make my bed, light the light.
I'll arrive, late tonight.
Blackbird, Bye, bye.

In his office Chubby got into his chair and made a face because it hurt him so much to sit down. He hung his cane over the arm of the chair and took a little while to get his breath while he opened a brown envelope and took out some papers.

"He shouldn't have pushed you off the front steps," he said to me, looking over his glasses. He was talking about my first day at school.

"Yes, sir."

"Did he hurt you?" He took his glasses off and slowed down his puffing.

"No, sir."

81

"He shouldn't have done that, you know. That wasn't fair."

"No, sir."

"You were doing a handstand." He put his glasses back on.

"Yes, sir."

"Did you make the gym team?"

"Yes, sir."

"Good for you," he said, and coughed a few times. "I have a happy thing to tell you. I have a very pleasant job to do here. I have something to say to you that you will be very pleased about. And your mother . . . your guardian, Mrs. O'Driscoll — she'll be very pleased about it too."

"Yes, sir," I said. I was getting sick of saying yes, sir, but that was all I could think of.

"He didn't hurt you when he pushed you down the stairs?"

"No, sir."

"I have a very pleasant duty to perform this morning. A legal matter. A person has asked me to deliver to you a cheque on this day, the last day of the month, a cheque for fifty dollars. I cannot give you the name of the person who directed me to give you this cheque. The only thing I can say to you is that for every month you stay in school, this school, you will receive a cheque for fifty dollars."

Chubby sighed as if he had just lifted a big weight and then passed over to me with his fat fingers a piece of paper.

"That is a cheque," he said, "for fifty dollars. On the last day of each month I'll be giving you a cheque for this amount. You will come into my office here and pick up the cheque on that day. It's not from me, you understand, although I sign it."

I couldn't stop thinking about the humming in the English teacher's room and the Hi-Y guys. The office was quiet except for a clock ticking. I got my mind away from the English teacher and the Hi-Y guys and looked at the cheque Chubby had pushed over his smooth desk at me.

The cheque said this:

Royal Bank of Canada
Pay to the order of Hulbert O'Driscoll
The sum of Fifty Dollars.

And then it said;

W.D.T. Atkinson (In Trust)

"What do I do with this?" I said.

"You go and cash it," said Chubby. "I'll give you a letter of identification, signed by me, that you keep with you to show to the bank so they will cash the cheque for you. And another letter to Mrs. O'Driscoll, explaining that she will be your adviser about how to handle this sudden windfall."

At the Royal Bank on Bank Street they read the letter, phoned Chubby at the school, talked to each other about it, pointed at me, had a little meeting, brought the manager out of his office, had another meeting, looked at my clothes, phoned somebody else, filled out some forms, stamped about ten pieces of paper, counted out the money in tens, started smiling, put the money in an envelope, licked the envelope, smiled some more, and gave it to me.

I folded the envelope in half, put it in my pocket, and walked down Bank Street, over the bridge, past the Mayfair Theatre, down the hill to the Uplands Bus Terminal, and got on the bus.

With my hand still in my pocket covering the envelope I sat down beside one of the rich people and rode home.

All I could think of the whole time was what Chubby had said.

"Sudden windfall," he said.

"Lord strike me dead," Mrs. O'Driscoll said. "Sudden windfall all right!"

We sat down at the kitchen table and forgot all about supper. Mrs. O'Driscoll got out the photograph album and we looked at some pictures of O'Driscoll. In all the pictures he was standing there, legs apart, hands on his hips, his shirt open, his hat tilted on one side.

We were talking about the money. Who could it be? Who was giving *us* this money?

Maybe it was Mr. O'Driscoll. It was just like him, Mrs. O'Driscoll was saying. Just like something he would do.

"That's just like something he would do. He probably didn't drown in the war after all. After he said, 'If I don't see you in the spring I'll see you in the mattress,' he jumped into the ocean and probably swam to some island or something and married the witchdoctor's daughter and became king and opened up a diamond mine and is a billionaire and feels so guilty that he's sending us fifty dollars every month. Just like something O'Driscoll would do. Swim to Africa or somewhere and move in with the Queen of the jungle and talk her out of all her gold and become a trillionaire and send us fifty dollars just to tease us. You can't fool me, O'Driscoll. I know it's you!"

Then she said some more about O'Driscoll and how he was probably living with the Queen of Sheba or somebody.

"Well, she can have him!" Mrs. O'Driscoll said. "She's welcome to him. And more power to her!"

Then Mrs. O'Driscoll said that O'Driscoll probably swam all the way to Hawaii or somewhere and moved in with some mermaid who had jewels in a chest sunk down in the ocean and convinced her to give him all her treasure, and he's now a multi-zillionaire and he's sending us fifty dollars.

"Is he sure he can spare it!" said Mrs. O'Driscoll out of the corner of her mouth.

But I stopped listening to Mrs. O'Driscoll because another idea was starting to come into my head. I started thinking about Miss Collar-Cuff. It was Miss Collar-Cuff who was giving me the money. Because of how sad she seemed to be. She probably wanted me to be her grandson, but she was afraid that I wouldn't and so she was giving me this money and keeping it a secret.

I was thinking that I might look right in her face next time and see if I could see in her eyes the secret she had. Or maybe I would tell her about getting the money and then watch her face to see if it said anything. To see if an expression came over her face that was different or if she looked away so I wouldn't be able to tell.

That's what I would do. I would tell her about Chubby giving me the cheque and see what she did. I would tell her maybe when she came in the room when I pretended to be asleep. When she came in to look for a long time at me when she thought I was asleep. Or when I was reading to her.

I went out in the hall to see if there was a lineup at the toilet. Mr. or Mrs. Blank must have been in there because Nerves was standing there staring at the door with his face all squeezed up.

I practiced on Nerves, pretending that Nerves was Miss Collar-Cuff.

"Somebody is giving me fifty dollars a month, but it's a secret," I said to Nerves. "Mrs. O'Driscoll thinks it's Mr. O'Driscoll, but it can't be. He was drowned in the war. It's not him. And it's not Chubby. It's somebody else. Do you know who it is?"

Nerves studied the floor for a while then raised his ratty little eyes slowly up to mine. His head was still down and his eyes were rolled up looking into mine. He was looking very mysterious.

Then he fell over and played dead.

What a dog.

Just then we both looked down the hall. A stranger was coming out of Mrs. Fitchell's unit. He didn't have black hair. He didn't have red hair. This one was bald.

12
Uppity

" $\mathbf{S}$ omebody is giving me, us, fifty dollars a month, but it's a secret," I said to Miss Collar-Cuff. "Mrs. O'Driscoll thinks it's Mr. O'Driscoll, but it can't be. He was drowned in the war. It's not him. It's somebody else. Chubby will give me a cheque for fifty dollars at the end of each month but he won't tell where it comes from."

I was reading to her from *War and Peace* when I said it. I stopped reading as I had planned, looked up over the book right at her eyes, and said it.

She looked at me for a long time before she answered.

"That's a wonderful thing, you and your mother receiving this money. The fact that you don't know where it's coming from might be a little disturbing, but, on the other hand, the source of this sudden windfall being anonymous might make this monthly allowance all the more pleasurable. What a fascinating mystery it is!"

What a sentence! It was just as long as some of the sentences in *War and Peace*. And she said "sudden windfall" just like Chubby did. And the sentence sounded like she had it planned. But her face showed nothing.

Then she said, "Now that you are a young man of means, do I assume that you will no longer remain in my employ and that I should begin searching for a replacement?"

"Oh, no, Miss," I said. "I have to stay at least until we finish *War and Peace!*"

"Ah, good, Hubbo, my friend. Although I doubt that we will last together *that* long. We will try our very best, won't we?"

The next Thursday from the big bed I tried again to get her to talk about the money but she just came out with a sentence even longer than before.

So I gave up.

One day Mrs. O'Driscoll and Fleurette and I discussed Denny's problem with Melody Bleach.

"Sounds like a hopeless case," said Mrs. O'Driscoll. "O'Driscoll used to be like that about me. Followed me around for about a year before I ever really noticed him. Wore out four pairs of shoes running after me, he told me later. I didn't believe him, though. He only had one pair of shoes as far as I ever knew. Of course, he was always exaggerating. You could never get the truth out of him. Denny will survive, though. Don't worry about him. Soon as his pimples go away, he'll be fine. And that Melody person. Really dumb, isn't she? Didn't you say she comes last in the class all the time?"

Mrs. O'Driscoll was right. Melody Bleach did always come in last. But what I didn't tell her was that Denny was coming second last. And he used to be so smart. Used to come at the top all the time.

What Mrs. O'Driscoll said about Denny's pimples gave me an idea. I would use some of the money to take Denny to a doctor and maybe get rid of his pimples. Make him feel better. More proud of himself.

On the way home a few days later I told Denny about the appointment I had made for him at the skin doctor. The dermatologist.

It wasn't hard to talk Denny into going to the appointment. He was in such a daze you could have told him to jump off the Bank Street Bridge into the canal and he would have.

Fleurette and I steered him down Fifth Avenue and into the doctor's waiting room. Everybody sitting around the waiting room was covered with pimples. We had never seen so many pimples.

"A lot of pimples in this room," whispered Fleurette.

They called Denny's name and he went in.

While we were waiting I started talking to Fleurette about the Boys' Hi-Y and my problems with the application.

"What do you want to join that stupid club for? Those morons keep walking through my school in their little gangs and their nice clothes making smart-alec remarks and bumping into the girls and laughing. They really think they're something but they're not. Everybody hates them. Except the girls who are really brainless. They like those Hi-Y guys because they have money. Take them out to restaurants and stuff. But you should hear what the Hi-Y guys say about the girls after, behind their backs. You're not going to be like that, are you?"

I didn't know what to say for a long time, so we sat in silence in the skin doctor's waiting room.

After a while, Denny came out with the doctor.

Fleurette and I looked at the doctor's face. He had more pimples than Denny. His face was a mess of scars and splotches.

"Now, apply this salve three times a day and take one of these pills every day after supper," the pimpled doctor was saying to Denny as I paid the nurse.

"It's sulphur," Denny told us later on the Uplands bus. Denny already had some of the salve on his face. It was skin-coloured and looked like makeup.

As the bus got warm I could start to smell the stuff. It was sulphur all right. It smelled like rotten eggs. In fact, Denny smelled quite a bit like Mr. Tool's stuffed owl.

We got off with him to have a visit and see what the Dorises thought of our plan to get rid of Denny's pimples. The Dorises were all sitting around the kitchen watching the potatoes and the kettle boil for supper.

All the Dorises agreed that something had to be done and everybody talked about pimples for a while, the history of pimples, the effects of pimples, how pimples can't *ruin* your life but can do a pretty good job trying to spoil everything.

The smell of rotten eggs from Denny's salve was getting worse. One of the Dorises told him to move away from the stove and maybe he'd be more comfortable.

"To be a success in life, you can't have pimples," I said. I said it, but it didn't sound like me. I could feel Fleurette's eyes go dark on me. I was starting to sound more and more like the guidance book.

"I suppose you couldn't join the Boys' Hi-Y if you had pimples," Fleurette said to me. Her black eyes were narrow and her lip was curled up. She was pretty mad at me about this Hi-Y stuff, I could tell.

Everybody talked some more about Denny's disease, and just before Fleurette and I left the oldest Doris piped up with something new.

"If this sulphur doesn't work we'll try the sand."

Sand?

"A teaspoon of clean sand every Saturday night. Boil the sand, take a big teaspoon of it every Saturday night after your bath, with a glass of warm milk to wash it down. Cured all of those things in my day."

Everybody said that this would be worth a try, and then Fleurette and I left to walk home to Uplands Emergency Shelter.

"Why did you say that about success and pimples? You sounded like somebody in that stupid guidance book. And why are you trying to join that awful club with those awful people? And Mrs. O'Driscoll told me that you're getting pretty uppity since you started getting that money. Maybe *you* should go to the doctor and get some of that rotten egg salve to put on your brain."

She never said another word and when we got into Building Eight she slammed the door.

Only Nerves was there in the hall. With his nose up in the air. He was mad at me too.

13
Feel Street

It was coming up to Christmas and the teachers were getting us ready for exams. In science we were doing the grasshopper all over again.

I was drawing those hairs or whatever they are on the grasshopper's tibia or his femur or whatever that part of his leg is called, when I heard some pounding at the front of the room. When I looked to see what all the fuss was about I noticed that Mr. Tool had gone berserk. He was pounding his head on the blackboard. His forehead, bang-banging on the blackboard. Then he picked up the cage with the snake in it and fired it across the room. Then he started ripping his charts down off the rollers and throwing test tubes at the class and at the windows. The Hi-Y guys had driven him crazy.

Then he tore two or three spouts off the sinks, and the water gushed up to the ceiling.

"I hate you!" he was screaming at us. "I hate you!" he was screaming while he threw some of his little dead experimental pigs at the class.

Then he picked up his horse skull and threw it through the glass windows of the cabinet where his stinking owl was sitting there glassy-eyed, staring at him. Then he picked up the owl and started ripping the feathers out of it. Then he started throwing all his stuffed rodents and the little logs and tree limbs they were stuck to out the window.

Then the vice-principal came in and started talking to him and taking him out, and Mr. Tool was saying, ". . . how can I go now, the period isn't over. I have to teach them the grasshopper . . . they have to know the grasshopper for the exam. Did the bell ring? Where's the bell? They don't know their work . . . what am I going to do? I hate them . . . don't you see? I hate these students. I want to kill them, kill them and put them in bottles on the window sill . . . put them in formaldehyde . . . cut them up in pieces and give them to my fish . . . kill . . . kill . . . kill!"

He was pretty mad at us.

School got out early because that day they had a sock hop, which was a little dance in the gym with your shoes off and just your socks on. We went and stood along the wall and sat along the wall on the long benches and leaned up against the wall where the mats were hanging, leaning on the mats at the sock hop against the wall.

Sliding our socks on the glistening floor.

In the middle of the floor the head boy and the head girl were dancing. The record that was playing was the song "Dream."

On the other side of the gym the girls were standing around talking in little bunches and leaning against the wall and the mats and standing there in their socks and laughing and covering their lips with their fingers.

The head of the Girls' Hi-Y turned the record over and played the song, "Golden Earrings."

The head girl and the head boy were out there dancing again.

One of the Hi-Y guys tried to shove me out on the floor and we had a bit of a wrestling match.

There were quite a few wrestling matches along our wall.

Then we saw Melody Bleach walk in, not clicking, and stand by herself. She touched her hair a bit, pushed it a bit with her fingertips every few minutes. She didn't look so scary without her high heels on.

Then we saw Denny walking across the floor toward her. Everybody was watching Denny. He was walking all wrong. When his right leg went out, so did his right arm. And then his left leg went out at the same time as his left arm. Everybody waited to see what would happen to him. When he got to her, he must have asked her for a dance. We saw her shake her head.

No.

Then Denny walked all the way back across the floor. It was a long walk. The floor seemed as big as the parade square at Uplands. Right leg, right arm. Left leg, left arm.

Poor Denny.

I left the dance and went to meet Fleurette at the Commerce door.

I had talked it over with Mrs. O'Driscoll and she had said it was a good idea.

I was going to buy Fleurette a present with some of the mysterious money.

I had on new underwear and new pants and new socks and shoes and a new shirt. Spoiling everything, I had on my long old raggedy coat and my galoshes with the soles flapping and the missing buckles.

We walked down cold Rideau Street and went into A. J. Freiman's. The heat blasted us in the swinging doors. We went up to the third floor on the elevator. The elevator lady had on a braided uniform and a cute cap and she called out what was on each floor and then opened the two doors by pulling down the handle with her red-gloved hand and saying, "Watch your step, please," but we didn't have to watch our step because she hit it right on.

They kept the girls' clothes on the third floor.

Over in the shoe department Fleurette told the man she wanted to try on some blue and white saddle shoes.

I saw the mother of a guy named Eddie I used to go to York Street School with. She was working in the girls' dress department. She saw me coming over and came to meet me a bit. She asked me what I was doing in the girls' clothing department, and I told her that a friend and I were buying some new clothes for her.

"Isn't that nice," she said. "Clothes are expensive these days." I could tell that she was, in a kind way, really asking where we got the money.

"I saw you come in," she said. "I think I know your friend. Doesn't she live around Friel Street somewhere? Pretty girl. I've seen her."

"We don't live in Lowertown anymore," I said. "We moved to Uplands Emergency Shelter. We got some money from a man my aunt knows."

I knew it sounded strange when I said it. Eddie's mother raised her eyebrows a bit. I wouldn't have lied about it, but I didn't feel like trying to explain to her what I couldn't even explain to myself.

She was a nice lady, not too nosy, so we talked for a while about Lowertown and Uplands until Fleurette came over wearing her new shoes over her old woolen stockings and carrying her ripped galoshes and her coat. Then Eddie's mother took her over to look at some more things and they disappeared for a while. I felt sort of silly standing around in the girls' clothing department by myself. So I went over and played with the X-ray machine.

I stuck my foot in and pushed the button. I looked through the glass. I could see the bones of my feet. They were a kind of green colour.

When Fleurette Featherstone Fitchell came back she had on new blue and white saddle shoes, new pink lisle stockings, a new blue skirt, a new pink angora sweater and a new blue ribbon in her long curly black hair.

She stood in front of one of the tall triple mirrors and opened one of them a bit so she could see her back. Then she pulled the other one towards her a little so that she could see me looking at her. I turned the first part of the mirror so that I could see reflections of a million Fleurettes in the other mirrors getting further and further and smaller away.

They all looked beautiful.

A little way up Rideau Street, in front of the Chateau Laurier, we met Victor, the guy who ran the Tuck Shop, and his girlfriend, Virginia. Victor had on a silky-silver new bomber jacket with the white fur collar turned up, a set of shiny black earmuffs, a white silk scarf showing where his jacket was half zipped up, a pair of fur-lined gloves turned down so you could see the fur, smooth, light-grey gabardine draped slacks with a special stitched seam down the side, and open flight boots with the fuzzy white wool lining flashing when he walked.

He showed us his shiny-white even teeth as he passed by with Virginia.

Virginia had on a brown mink hat with the fur just down to her eyes, a long beige camelhair coat open at the throat showing her shiny necklace; the split in her coat made her long high-heeled cowhide black soft leather boots swish out when she walked. Her silver earrings glistened in the lights from the Chateau Laurier and the twinkling snow.

She showed us a big row of shiny-white even teeth as she passed by with Victor.

"Oh, my," said Fleurette Featherstone Fitchell. "Oh, my!", after they'd passed by. "That's one of those dopes that comes over to our school and bumps into us and everything."

We walked up to Rideau Street a little more, crossing Rideau Street Bridge, and stopped by Sir Galahad's statue in front of the Parliament Buildings.

Fleurette was looking straight ahead.

"How do they get teeth like that?" she said. "Do they buy them or what do they do? Are they false teeth or what? Maybe they paint them on or something. Maybe they're drawn on. Or they buy them at the joke shop or something. Bill's Joke Shop." She was talking like Mrs. O'Driscoll. Not talking sense. "My mother says it's their diet," Fleurette said. "What do they do, eat pearls for breakfast or something? Maybe they feed them oysters and grains of sand or . . . maybe they're injected with something . . . maybe they get ground-up diamonds and put it in their food."

She was in one of her Hi-Y moods.

As we were leaving the statue I saw a guy I sort of knew in Lowertown. His name was Tommy and he was with his friend Sammy. Fleurette and Tommy had a little conversation about Christmas. Fleurette was being really nice to him.

We went down Sparks Street to Bank Street and waited for the streetcar.

"Or maybe they take those sequins, those shiny things, and eat them in their cereal in the morning."

The streetcar came along and it was jammed and we jammed on.

"Maybe they're in the chiclet business. Maybe those are just chiclets!"

Fleurette Featherstone Fitchell calmed down a bit and smiled at me with her black eyes and after a while made me smile too and she put our two dimes in.

People were crowding and pushing, trying to get on and off at each stop while we moved deeper and deeper into the back of the streetcar. By the time we got to the Avenues we got a seat. By the time we got to Sunnyside Avenue by the Mayfair Theatre in Ottawa South and got up to get off, the car was only half full.

We got off at Coulter's Drug Store and started walking down the rest of Bank Street towards the Uplands Bus Terminal. The running lights from the Mayfair Theatre made shadows move on the snowbanks.

The Uplands Bus Terminal windows were dripping with dirt. Inside, the rich people were near the door and the poor people were lying on the benches and standing around with their broken parcels and their bags.

As we were getting off the bus at Uplands I was telling her something about Doug and Mr. Tool and going berserk and everything, and suddenly Fleurette Featherstone Fitchell stopped and turned.

"Doug!" she said. "Doug is the name of one of those guys that come over to our school with all those dirty sayings and grabbing at us! Doug is that slimy-looking guy with the grease on his head. Doug! That's your Hi-Y friend? That skinny, ugly guy! Do you know what he shouted at me last week? *Feel* Street! Did you used to live on *Feel* Street! You told him that! Nobody else knows that but you! You promised never to tell that!" She was screaming at me now. "*You* told him about Feel Street. What they said about me in Lowertown!"

"I didn't!" I said. "I didn't tell him anything about you. He was always asking me but I never said one word about you. Never!"

"You're a liar!" she screamed. "Nobody else knows that but you. It must have been you!"

"I didn't!" I said. "Honest to God, I didn't!"

"And I'm a liar too," she shouted. "Did you know that? The man with the black hair? He's my father all right! But he's not like I said. Remember the cast on my mother's wrist? And the man with the red hair? He's not my uncle! He's just a man. And there are other men who come over. And sometimes they bring presents or money. But I don't know who they are! They bring ribbons maybe! Like you!"

She was tearing the ribbon out of her hair.

"You told about Feel Street! You traitor!" she said between her teeth. Her eyes were black as coal. "You blabbed all over . . ."

She threw the ribbon down in the snow and stomped on it.

Then she hit me in the face. Then she ran to Building Eight.

"Is that what you do?" I yelled after her. "Hit people?"

That's all I could think of to say.

The next morning Mrs. O'Driscoll found all the new clothes in a pile in the hall outside our door.

14
Sixty-Four Pieces

All through Christmas and January and February and March Fleurette wouldn't talk to me.

In science Doug and some of the other Hi-Y troublemakers were moved to another class. I only saw Doug a couple of times in the boys' dressing room selling chocolate bars. Mrs. O'Driscoll said once she thought there was something funny going on about those chocolate bars and the Tuck Shop, but I didn't pay much attention to what she said.

At Miss Collar-Cuff's we were up to Book One Part Two of *War and Peace*, where two thousand Russian soldiers marched seven hundred miles to Austria and wore out their boots. That was four thousand worn-out boots. We were on page one hundred and twenty-five. One thousand three hundred pages to go.

Quite a big book.

One day I joined the library club and they gave me a job, one day a week after school, putting books back on the shelves.

One day in English class I told the teacher I was reading *War and Peace* by Leo Tolstoy. He kept me after class and told me that being a liar would never make me a success in life.

One day Melody Bleach quit school and soon Denny's pimples got a little better and so did his marks.

One day in guidance class I finished filling out the Hi-Y application form. Here's what it said.

NAME: Hulbert O'Driscoll
ADDRESS: 210 Easy Avenue
PHONE NUMBER: Central 34141 (Tuesdays and Thursdays only)
AMBITION: Brain Surgeon
EXPERIENCE IN CLUBS: Library Club
AWARDS: Glebe Gymnastics Sweater
TEAMS: Gym Team
FATHER'S OCCUPATION: Doctor and Lawyer
MAKE AND YEAR OF FATHER'S CAR: Brand-New Cadillac
RELIGION: Lutheran

After gymnastics that night, Doug was in the boys' dressing room selling chocolate bars.

"I'll make a deal with you," he said. "If you get that girl Fleurette to talk to me and get her to go out with me, I'll get you into the Hi-Y even without an application form."

"How did you know about Feel Street?" I said. I hated looking at his face.

"I was selling chocolate bars over at Lisgar Collegiate. There's a guy there, my chocolate-bar partner over there, he knows her. He told me."

"What guy?"

"A guy from where she used to go to school."

"What's his name?"

"Killer Bodnoff is his name," said Doug. "Will you do it? Get her to talk to me and I'll get you into the Hi-Y. No application form. I know your application form is a fake. I saw you put down 210 Easy

Avenue. I checked. You don't live there. An old lady lives there. Is it a deal? I can get you in."

"No, it's not a deal," I said. "You're stealing those chocolate bars, aren't you?"

"Prove it," said Doug, his eyebrow going up and down.

I had my application form in my pocket, and on the way home I stopped at the top of the Bank Street Bridge.

You can only tear a piece of paper in half six times. I took the Hi-Y application form out of my pocket and folded it in half. Then I tore it down the crease and put one piece exactly on the other. Then I tore them in half again. Now I had four pieces. Then I put the two pieces on top of the other two and tore again. Now I had eight. I did it again and had sixteen. Mrs. O'Driscoll once told me that no matter how big the piece of paper was, you could only tear it in half five or six times. If it was the size of Landsdowne Park or the size of Ottawa you could only tear it in half a half a dozen times or so. Then it would be too small to tear anymore.

I tore again and had thirty-two.

My fingers were hurting and I was swearing and crying, and I tore once more for sixty-four. That was all I could do. Mrs. O'Driscoll was right. Six times.

I threw the sixty-four pieces of the Hi-Y application form up in the air over the railing of the Bank Street Bridge.

They floated down like snowflakes and fluttered down on the broken black melting spring ice of the Rideau Canal.

15

Uranus

It was near the end of May.

The next day was a school holiday because of a teachers' convention so I was coming in on the Uplands bus in the afternoon to go to Miss Collar-Cuff's. It was a strange time of the day to be on the bus. It was very quiet. In fact, the only other person on the bus with me was Mrs. O'Driscoll, who was going shopping.

When we transferred to the streetcar in Ottawa South, Mrs. O'Driscoll suddenly said she had some extra time so she'd be able to get off at Easy Avenue and come down to Miss Collar-Cuff's with me for a short visit before she went ahead to do her shopping.

"Might as well have a look at her, see where my boy is spending a lot of his time," she said out of the corner of her mouth.

I had a feeling of terror that maybe Mrs. O'Driscoll would spoil everything. Maybe she'd go into one of her long speeches or something. Embarrass me. Start talking about O'Driscoll and the war or say something about the money. Or start singing.

"Maybe you haven't got time. Taking an extra streetcar might make you late for shopping," I said.

"I've got lots of time. Never been late for shopping in my life. Not gonna start now, Hubbo, I can tell you that for sure. How can you be late for shopping?"

"Maybe Miss Collar-Cuff will be asleep. You won't be able to see her," I said.

"Yasso?" said Mrs. O'Driscoll, making a joke. "Let me worry about that. At least I'll be able to have a look at this awful fancy house of hers. Give her some tips. Rearrange her furniture for her." She gave me an elbow in the ribs. She was in a very good mood.

"Sometimes she just sits there. She won't even talk," I said, still trying to discourage her. "She never has visitors," I said.

The streetcar was close now. Two stops to go before Easy Avenue.

Mrs. O'Driscoll was all of a sudden quiet and I could feel her stiffen up as I leaned over to ring the bell. She had an expression on her face that didn't look like her. A blank expression. Looking straight ahead. Her hat straight on her head. She was almost like a photograph. Her eyes looking at nothing. Sitting straight in her seat. Her hands folded in her lap.

"Please don't come," I heard myself say.

Then the photograph spoke.

"You're afraid you might be ashamed of me, is that it, Hubbo?" said the photograph.

"No! No, it's just that . . . "

"Well, don't you worry about it. I wouldn't do that to you. There'll be time to meet your Miss Collar-Cuff. Anyway, you're right. I might be late for shopping. You'd better get going. This is your stop, isn't it?"

The streetcar driver was looking at me in his mirror. Was I going to get off or what?

"Go on. I'll see you tomorrow," said Mrs. O'Driscoll.

I got off and watched the streetcar move along the track. I gave a little wave as Mrs. O'Driscoll's window went by. She didn't look. She was staring straight ahead with that expression I had never seen before.

I felt like diving under the wheels of the streetcar and getting crushed.

I walked slowly down Easy Avenue and went into her rich house there. Miss Collar-Cuff was sitting reading while I hung up my coat and then went into the kitchen to make her some tea.

After a few sips of tea she put down her cup and said something that made my heart jump.

"Well," she said, "one of these times you must bring your Mrs. O'Driscoll over for a little visit. I'd very much like to meet her."

"Yes, Miss," I said to Miss Collar-Cuff. "Would next Thursday be okay?"

After I read to her a little bit from *War and Peace* she fell asleep in her chair. I got up quietly and went into the den to spend some time with the books in there. About half an hour later I went back into the living room to see if she wanted more tea but she was still asleep. The fire was almost out so I went out to the garage to get some wood. I opened and closed the driver's door of the Cadillac a few times to hear it chunk and I sat behind the wheel for a while.

When I came back in she was standing up, leaning on the back of her big chair. Her face was very tight and her lips were pressed together. And her eyes were staring straight ahead and glassy, like the lion's eyes. I put my shoulder under her arm and my arm around her back and we went up the stairs together to her bedroom.

Then I went back downstairs and phoned her nurse.

I brought her some tea and cookies upstairs and then some juice and later some ice water but she didn't want any of it. She dozed off while I read to her some more, and I tucked her in a bit and turned out her light and went downstairs to answer the door. It was the nurse, and after she went up to see Miss Collar-Cuff she came down and told me I might as well go home. She was going to call the doctor and stay the night.

When I got home I told Mrs. O'Driscoll Miss Collar-Cuff was sick. Mrs. O'Driscoll didn't say much. She just gave me my supper and then went right to bed.

The next day in science we were reviewing the grasshopper for the final exam and also talking about the planet Uranus and how the days on Uranus are forty-two years long and so are the nights. It was pretty interesting. The new teacher was telling us how the planet turned so slowly that the days and nights were forty-two years long. The planet Earth was really spinning around quickly compared to Uranus. Here the days and nights were only about twelve hours each. I was thinking some crazy things about life on earth and how fast it was. Go to bed. Sleep. Get up. Live. Go to bed. Sleep. Get up. Live.

"No wonder nobody lives there," some of the leftover Hi-Y guys were saying. "What if you stayed up all night with your girlfriend? Your parents would probably be dead by the time you got home!"

"Shut up, you stupid boys," our new teacher was saying when the phone rang.

"O'Driscoll you're wanted in the main office," he said, while the leftover Hi-Y guys were trying to stab the fish in the aquarium with their compasses.

Chubby was sitting behind his desk with a sad look on his face.

"Hubbo, my boy," said Chubby, "I have some very sad news to report to you. Miss Collar-Cuff passed away in her sleep last night. Her nurse called me this morning and told me."

I guess some tears came to my eyes because Chubby got out of his chair in his rumpled old suit and came around the desk without his cane and with pain on his face and put his arm on my shoulder and gave me a few pats. I felt my shoulder where he had put his hand.

"You liked her, didn't you?" said Chubby.

"Yes," I said, "I did."

"She was a very lonely lady," said Chubby.

Chubby was a very kind-hearted man.

Then he looked at me for a long time as if he was going to tell me something more. But he didn't. After a little chat about death and how it's good to die peacefully, in your sleep, with no pain, he said, "Now I have another unpleasant duty to perform. I have to see about some stealing that's been going on down at the Tuck Shop. You'd better go back to class now."

Back in class, while the Hi-Y guys were firing fish around the room, I was thinking about how long the nights were on Uranus and how short they were here on earth and how much can happen in one short night. How one short night can change everything.

Sleep. Get up. Live. Go to bed. Sleep. Die.

No more.

During gymnastics that day I felt sick and told the coach I was leaving a bit early.

On the Uplands bus the seat beside Mr. Yasso was empty but I went right past it and stood at the back the whole way home. In Building Eight I went right to the toilet and locked the door. I was trying to be sick but I couldn't. I sat in there for a while until I heard somebody try the door. Then I heard some talking. It was Mrs. O'Driscoll and Fleurette.

They didn't know I was in there.

They were talking about me.

Fleurette was talking to Mrs. O'Driscoll about what a drip I'd been since we got the money. How mean I was being and how snooty I was getting and how I was hanging around with those dopey Hi-Y guys. And Mrs. O'Driscoll was saying that I was acting a little strange and hurtful and how if O'Driscoll was here he'd sit me down and give me a bit of a talking to and straighten me out. Then I heard Fleurette go down the hall and I heard her door shut.

I called through the door as the tears came.

"Mrs. Collar-Cuff died," I called, half choking.

Out in the hall there was dead silence.

"Hubbo, my boy," I heard Mrs. O'Driscoll say.

I opened the door.

We were staring at each other.

Suddenly we were both talking and putting our arms around each other and patting each other and saying how sorry we were and saying everything would be all right and there, there and that's okay now.

"Oh, Hubbo," Mrs. O'Driscoll was saying, "I'm so sorry that I acted the fool. I should have gone to see her yesterday. It was so mean of me and so childish of me to do what I did. Not going to see her like that. Oh, Hubbo, please forgive me. Oh, Hubbo, don't feel bad. You're a good boy. Everything will be all right."

And even Nerves was there, putting his paws on my leg.

In the paper the next day it said that Miss Collar-Cuff had deceased and that she had no relatives and that she would be cremated because that was what was in her will.

16
A Deal With Doug

After gymnastics a few days later I was alone at my locker and the hall was empty.

Suddenly Doug came running up and his ugly face looked sick. He fumbled around with his combination lock with his long bony fingers and then tore open his locker.

"Quick," he said. "I'll make a deal with you." He took out a box of forty-eight chocolate bars from his locker. "Put these in your locker and I'll get you into the Hi-Y for sure. No questions asked. My brother told me Chubby and the vice-principal are coming down right now to search my locker! If they find these I'm done for! Quick!"

"I'll make a deal with you," I said. "You tell Fleurette Featherstone Fitchell who told you about Feel Street and I'll do it. I don't want to be in your stupid club."

"It's a deal!" he said.

I grabbed the box and shoved it under my gymnastics stuff in the bottom of my locker. Doug locked his locker and ran into the boy's can to hide just as Chubby came puffing down the stairs and the vice-principal behind him. I left my locker open and started piling up some books to take home.

Chubby said hello to me and the vice-principal took out the combination number he had written down and checked the locker number and opened up Doug's locker. They searched all through his locker and then shook their heads and closed it up again.

"Somebody's been stealing from the Tuck Shop," Chubby told me. "We think it's this fellow but we can't prove it. Do you know anything about it, Hubbo?"

I looked straight in Chubby's face. The vice-principal was behind him, his face hanging there. He seemed even bigger than ever. He must have been still growing or something.

"No, I don't, sir," I said to Chubby. My face felt funny and my lips felt thick and rubbery.

Chubby looked at me for a minute and then they went back upstairs. When they were gone Doug came out of the can and I gave him the stolen box of chocolate bars.

"Now, you'll come home with me and you'll tell Fleurette."

"I'll tell her later," said Doug.

"No, now!" I said.

"Maybe I will, maybe I won't," said Doug. "It's your word against mine now anyway!"

"My mother knows Chubby. She has proof. She saw you. I'll squeal on you and so will she."

"Your mother?"

"My mother is Mrs. O'Driscoll, the cleaning lady. He'll believe her. They're friends."

"Who's going to believe you and a cleaning lady?" said Doug.

All I could see was Doug's eyebrow. I felt like my mouth was full of blood.

The next thing I knew he was on the floor, his nose gushing out red. I had punched him so hard my hand felt like it was broken. I had never hit anybody in my life before. It scared me so much I started to shake. I used to fight in Angel Square all the time, but that was just for fun. I never hit anybody. I reached down and grabbed him by the wrist and twisted his arm behind his back so that he had to stand up. I knew how to do it because I had watched the Uplands bus driver do that to some of the passengers who couldn't behave on his bus late at night.

I twisted his arm so far up his back that he had to walk. I walked him down First Avenue that way and down Bank Street. Over the Bank Street Bridge I felt like breaking his arm and throwing him in the canal.

At the bus terminal the bus was just leaving and I shoved him on and made him pay our fares.

"Got yourself a prisoner?" the driver said.

Mr. Yasso was on the bus and the seat beside him was empty. I pushed Doug into the seat and we took off. His shirt was covered with blood and he was crying.

"I'm taking this guy home with me to confess to something he did," I told Mr. Yasso.

"Yasso?" said Mr. Yasso. He smelled worse than he ever smelled before.

When we got to Building Eight, Mrs. O'Driscoll and Fleurette were standing outside.

"Well, well," said Mrs. O'Driscoll, "what have we here? It's our Hubbo with a friend with blood all over him. It's the snot who steals from the Tuck Shop, is it?"

Fleurette was standing there with her mouth open.

"Tell her," I said to Doug. "Tell her about Feel Street," I said, "or I'll break your arm!"

Mrs. O'Driscoll had her chin stuck out and she was standing close to Doug, staring him in the face. She had her hands on her hips. The look she had on her was going to turn Doug to stone.

111

Then Doug started blubbering and saying that it was Killer Bodnoff who told him about Feel Street and that I never said anything to him about Fleurette no matter how many times he tried to ask me, and please would Mrs. O'Driscoll not tell Chubby about what he did.

Then Mrs. O'Driscoll made a little speech as Fleurette slipped her hand inside mine.

"You young scalliwag, you're going to be leaving my home in the next thirty seconds, but before you go you're going to listen to this. I know you've been stealing stuff from the Tuck Shop and selling it because I've seen you. I'm a very good friend of Mr. Chubby and I'm going to decide tonight when I go to bed whether I'm going to tell him about that tomorrow or not. So you go home and think about that tonight. And think about this too. Think about why rich boys like you steal. Think about that. If O'Driscoll was here he'd kick you down the stairs. If we had any stairs! Now get your ugly face out of here!"

Then we went inside and left him standing there.

We watched out the window as Doug walked over with his head down to wait for the bus.

"I shouldn't have hit him," I said.

Fleurette was holding my hand. She said she hoped in her heart all along that I had never told Doug anything about her. Then she gave me a little kiss on the part of my face where she hit me. Her eyes were a soft brown colour.

Then Mrs. O'Driscoll sang a bit of "Bye, Bye, Blackbird," and then we went into the kitchen and had a meeting to organize a big picnic Mrs. O'Driscoll wanted us to have at the sandpits to celebrate the end of school.

17
Just Like Something O'Driscoll Would Do

It was the end of June and there was one day of school left. I went to see Chubby to see if there was a cheque waiting for me as usual. I didn't really think there would be one because I was more and more sure that it was Miss Collar-Cuff who was the secret moneygiver the whole time and now that she was . . . I couldn't even say the word.

Chubby was sitting behind his desk. He looked better than usual. Except for his suit. His face seemed brighter and he wasn't puffing like he often did. I think it was because school was over and now he could go for a two month's rest all summer.

When I asked Chubby about the cheque he got a very serious look on his face.

"Due to recent circumstances, of which you are sadly aware, the arrangement concerning your monthly expectations, as it has been up to this point in time, has ceased," he said.

Whatever that meant. It was the kind of sentence Miss Collar-Cuff used every time I ever tried to ask her about the money. Anyway, I said good-bye to Chubby and told him I would miss him over the summer.

"You'll be back in the fall, I presume?" he asked.

"Yes, I will," I said.

"Good," he said. "That will make everything just fine then."

I had one more thing to do.

Everybody was crowded around the Tuck Shop and around the lockers getting packed up for the summer. Everybody was in a good mood. Laughing and singing and joking around.

I stayed by my locker, hiding behind the open door. I was waiting for Mrs. O'Driscoll to come by the same time she usually did.

Right on time, I saw her coming down the hall, pushing her pail in front of her with the mop in it like she always did.

When she got near my open locker I stepped out in front of her and stopped her.

I took the mop handle out of her hand and put my arms around her and gave her a big hug in front of everybody.

A big cheer went up and everybody started laughing and hugging each other and slapping us on the back.

Mrs. O'Driscoll's lips were on my ear.

"Oh, Hubbo," she whispered to me, "you're just like O'Driscoll. This is what he would have done too. This is exactly what he would have done!"

I felt good.

I walked out of Glebe Collegiate Institute, and all the way down First Avenue I wondered why Chubby was acting a little strange. First the Miss Collar-Cuff sentence and then saying "Make everything just fine then," was bothering me a bit.

On the way over the Bank Street Bridge some of the Uplands kids were throwing their school books and papers in the canal. Some of them really hated school a lot.

After Mrs. O'Driscoll got home she and Fleurette started getting ready for the picnic. Mrs. O'Driscoll kept saying that it *wasn't* Miss Collar-Cuff that was giving us the money, it was O'Driscoll the whole time, and this *proved* it was O'Driscoll.

"*What* proves it was O'Driscoll?" I said.

"The fact that he *didn't* send it this month!" said Mrs. O'Driscoll. "Don't you see? That's just like something he'd do! That's just like him to start sending some money every month and then just as you start getting used to it—he forgets to send it! The whole idea! It's perfect O'Driscoll! Forget all about his responsibilities! Start something and then don't finish it! Probably gave the money to some floozy in New Zealand or somewhere!"

"What's a floozy?" I asked. Fleurette and I were laughing.

"Never mind what a floozy is, but don't you see? It's exactly like something O'Driscoll would go and do! Start something and not finish it! Started in the war—couldn't even finish that—had to swim off somewhere! Well, she can have him, whoever she is, and the money too! Typical O'Driscoll. Oh, it's him all right! Probably too tied up with that Egyptian princess he was likely staying with to remember a small detail like sending us the fifty dollars. What he needs is a good swift kick!"

Mrs. O'Driscoll had to stop talking about this for a second so she could take a big breath and start saying some more about O'Driscoll.

She sure had a lot to say when it came to the subject of O'Driscoll.

In a little while Denny Dingle came in and said that on our way to the sandpits we could stop by and pick up some of the Dorises because they were coming with us too.

Then he helped us pack some of the picnic stuff: the homemade bread, the peanut butter and the honey, the weiners, the oranges, the butter, the

115

pickles and the mustard and the grape juice and the blankets and the boiled eggs and the cups and the salt and pepper and some plates and a knife.

And Mrs. O'Driscoll's sherry.

And my *War and Peace*.

Then Fleurette and Denny went around to the other units and got Mr. and Mrs. Blank and Nerves and Mr. Yasso and Mrs. Stentorian.

And Mrs. Fitchell.

While we were all gathered around outside Building Eight, getting our stuff organized and getting ready to walk down to the sandpits, a big fancy car pulled up.

Out of the car got Mr. Donald D. Donaldmcdonald!

He came right over to me and put his hand on my shoulder just like he did one time before. It seemed so long ago.

Then I knew!

I knew it was him. I knew he was the one who was the secret moneygiver.

And then he explained everything.

He was Miss Collar-Cuff's lawyer. He got me the job with her.

"I knew she would like you. She tried others but they didn't work out. But I knew you would. And the fifty dollars a month. That's for your education. To help you with it."

Then he handed me a cheque.

"Here's this month's cheque. It's signed by me now because it's not a secret anymore. Before, I had Miss Collar-Cuff to keep an eye on your schooling. But you'll do fine from now on. How's *War and Peace* going?"

He said a whole lot of other things about Chubby and about how I saved his life and how he quit playing golf to try and let off steam, and everybody was excited and Nerves was running around like he was on fire and Mrs. O'Driscoll was crying.

And I won't tell you what Mr. Yasso said when I got around to introducing him to Mr. Donald D. Donaldmcdonald.

We all walked out the gate with our stuff (Mr. Donald D. Donaldmcdonald left his car there and walked with us) and walked along the air strip and past the Ottawa Hunt and Golf Club where I was remembering how the early morning sun used to be on the wet putting green glistening silver off the dew. The green slopes down and the fairway rolls away down into the mist and then comes up again soft and green.

The little tin flags sticking up out of the holes on the putting green. And a spider string or two, beads of dew glistening down on them.

And maybe there's one golfer out there practicing his putting, the ball making little rainbows when it plows its little way, throwing up a spray in the early morning.

The smell of sweet-sweet-warm-plant-juice-cut-grass. And the smell of the pine all around and the chuckling of the chipmunks, and then the crunch of somebody coming around the corner from the pro shop, crunching on the crushed stone path with the golf spikes like hearing somebody eating cornflakes.

On the way to the sandpits we stopped and picked up a few of the Dorises.

At the sandpits the sun was high and hot now, and everything was clear as in a photograph.

All of us sitting and lying around the blankets. The pots and dishes and stuff spread around the little smouldering fire. The smoke floating, curling softly in graceful shapes. The sand cliff rising behind us, golden brown sugar. The top of the sandpit, so far up there and so clear. The fine edge of it like gold steel against the sky.

And Mrs. O'Driscoll, standing now, staring up there, pointing.

Pointing at a figure standing away up there, legs apart, hands on his hips, his shirt open, his sun hat tilted on one side.

Mrs. O'Driscoll's mouth opening, dropping her glass of sherry in the sand, trying to say these words.

Then saying these words:

"Lord strike me dead!"

And then these words:

"It's O'Driscoll!"

SOME OF THE CHARACTERS

Hubbo — a boy with success on his mind

Mr. Donald D. Donaldmcdonald — the world's worst golfer

Mrs. O'Driscoll — a lady to whom life is just like a song

O'Driscoll — a man who is missing

Mrs. Fitchell — a mother with a cast on her wrist

Fleurette Featherstone Fitchell — a girl who is proud though she wears a rag in her long curly black hair

Nerves — a dog who should have been a mirror

Mr. and Mrs. Blank — people who see themselves in their pet's face

Denny Dingle — a boy who was the victim of pimples

The Dorises — one big happy family

Mr. Tool — a teacher driven berserk by his students

Doug — a sneaky Hi-Y guy

Chubby — a man in pain but kind at the same time

Mr. Yasso — a rotten conversationalist

Mr. Stentorian — a man on the night shift

Mrs. Stentorian — a woman living a life of constant thunder

Miss Collar-Cuff — a rich lady and alone

the grasshopper — an insect studied to death

Mr. Stubbs — a man who travels a lot

Lassie — a success

Melody Bleach — a hypnotist

the English teacher — he keeps you from reading too much

Victor and Virginia — people with award-winning teeth

the dermatologist — a doctor who can't cure himself

Other books by Brian Doyle

Hey, Dad!

Megan can't imagine anything worse than a trip with her parents and often painful younger brother, when she really wants to stay at home and be president of the "Down With Boys Club." But she has to go.

This is the story of that trip and of how Megan learns to talk to her dad. But first she has to run away.

I.S.B.N. 0-88899-004-9 $6.95

You Can Pick Me Up at Peggy's Cove

"What would you do if your dad ran away from home?

Well, I was sent to spend the summer at Peggy's Cove. Part of the time I was really happy, and part of the time I was sad, and worried, and scared. I wrote my dad a long letter; I learned how to fish; I almost got into big trouble, and a whole lot more. Most of all I wanted my dad to come and pick me up at Peggy's Cove."

You Can Pick Me Up At Peggy's Cove is a sequel to *Hey, Dad!*

I.S.B.N. 0-88899-001-4 $6.95

Up to Low

In *Up to Low*, Young Tommy and Baby Bridget, the girl with trillium-shaped eyes, discover that loving and healing and dying are not always what they seem. And they make the discovery with the help of a wonderful cast of characters, including Crazy Mickey, drunken Frank, and the Hummer.

Up to Low was winner of the 1983 Canadian Library Association Book of the Year Award.

I.S.B.N. 0-88899-017-0 $6.95

Angel Square

All over Angel Square, Catholics, Protestants and Jews are tearing the sleeves out of one another's coats and trying to rip each other limb from limb.

Suddenly the bells from the three schools begin to ring.

Priests and teachers are running, herding people back to their own buildings.

There is a lot of shouting and bawling. It is like runaway cattle in a movie.

Soon the square will be empty.

Only hundreds of mitts and hats and parts of coats will be left, dark patches in the white snow.

Young Tommy, aka The Shadow, is seeing Angel Square through new eyes. Someone who hates Jews has beaten up his best friend's father, and beaten him up for real. The Shadow won't rest until he finds out who did it.

Award-winning author Brian Doyle brings his powerful blend of humour and wisdom to bear in this mystery which confronts the issue of racial hatred.

I.S.B.N. 0-88899-070-7 $4.95